BROKEN
Promises

The Broken Road Series, Book 2

MELISSA HUIE

Editorial provided by BookIvy Word Studio http://bookivyediting.com

Proof reading provided by M. K. Martin, Emma Mack, Ultra Editing – www.ultraeditingco.com

Formatting – Pink Ink Designs www.pinkinkdesigns.com

Cover Design by Robin Harper, Wicked by Design: wickedbydesigncovers.com

Front Cover Photography: Sara Eirew: saraeirew.com

Back Cover Photography by James Sasser: facebook.com/sasserfrazphotography

Back Cover Models – William Scott with his son, Will: facebook.com/WilliamScott55555

Author Photography by Cassy Roop, Pink Ink Designs - http://www.pinkinkdesigns.com

Previously self-published 2014, and published with BookTrope in 2015.

ISBN-10: 0-9980511-1-X

ISBN-13: 978-0-9980511-1-6

Library of Congress Control Number: 2015913532

Love Until Forever Ends.

Melissa Huie

BROKEN
Promises

CHAPTER 1

A M I DREAMING?

I'd been having a lot of wicked dreams lately. You know the kind, dreams that seem so real your breath quickens and your heart pounds. But I was pretty sure I wasn't dreaming as I stood in the driveway as drops of water bounced off my nose, the cold rain stinging my skin and plastering my shirt to my body. But dreaming was the only explanation I could fathom. How else could I have been standing in the middle of the street in the middle of the night five feet away from a man that everyone believed was dead? I had been dreaming of this man for the last five months. The father of my yet-to-be-born daughter, the man who'd had my heart for the past ten years, was standing under the cover of my carport right in front of me. His body was thinner and drawn, his clothes ragged and dirty. His hair was longer and curled at the ends. But his eyes—his eyes were the same shade of beautiful hazel.

"Shane!" His name came out more like a strangled cry. I rushed up the driveway to him, expecting him to disappear, as he had done in all my other dreams. The hard wall of his chest bounced me back and his strong arms held me tight. I brushed my sopping wet hair out of my eyes and looked up at him, searching for...I didn't know what. Maybe something, anything to confirm that this was another one of my nightmares and that I had completely lost my mind. Instead, he met my gaze with his intense stare. Warmth flooded through me and hope dared to show its head. *If this is a dream, I don't ever want to wake up.*

"Please tell me this is real. I can't handle this if it's not real."

"Baby, if you're dreaming, so am I," Shane rasped, his voice husky and thick with emotion. His arms hardened around me even more. "Thank God you're okay. I wouldn't have been able to live with myself if something had happened to you." His lips crushed mine. The heat from his kiss, so hot and intense, sent a bolt of electricity down to my toes.

I threw my arms around his neck and pulled him into me, pressing myself as close to him as I could. *Oh my God. He's here. He's really here.* Practically gasping for air, I looked at him in awe. "I can't believe it. You're here!" I stuttered.

"I'm here, Baby, and I'm never leaving you again. Let's go inside. You're freezing," he murmured. He led me from the cold of the night through the side entrance and into the warmth of the mudroom where a basket of fresh towels sat on top of the dryer.

"What happened? Are you hurt? Are you okay? They told me…I never thought…I mean…The police couldn't find…But I always knew…" I stammered. I couldn't form a complete sentence, a complete thought. My body trembled, but I needed him to know that I never gave up. That I still loved him and had always thought of him. Shane took a towel and briskly rubbed my shoulders and arms as I stood there in a daze. Sensing my disorientation, he wrapped the towel around me and crushed me to his chest. His hazel eyes burned through mine as he cupped my face with his hands.

"I couldn't get to you fast enough. Every path I took led me farther and farther away from you. I don't how I made it back. The only thing that kept me going was the hope that you were all right. I love you so much. You don't know…you just don't know how you kept me going," he whispered, lowering his head to mine.

The feel of his lips, the heat of his breath, pulsed through me like a shot of lightning. I shrugged off my towel and threw my arms around him, responding with everything I had. The pain of losing him, the overwhelming joy of seeing him, the desire that had been suppressed for so long—all these emotions washed over me like a waterfall. I held onto him as if he would disappear at any moment.

His tongue caressed mine like a familiar dance partner, breathtaking and sensual. My pulse raced. My blood boiled. His muscular arms held me against his body, as close as possible with this basketball between us. I mentally groaned. It was difficult to keep him close, and the more I tried, the more awkward it felt. Despite our emotions running high, we couldn't ignore the elephant in the room.

Shane broke off the kiss with a slight chuckle. "I guess we have some talking to do." Then he noticed my chattering teeth and stopped. "I'll be right back," he said, and hurried out of the mudroom.

What just happened? Where is he going? Before I could muster up a possible explanation, he bounded down the stairs with my bathrobe. He put his hands down at the hem of my shirt and then thought twice.

"May I?" he asked with hesitation in his voice. I nodded, too cold to speak. I desperately tried to figure out a way to say, "Surprise! You're a father!"

Shane lifted my shirt over my head. I watched his eyes rove over my body. I was exposed, physically and emotionally. Standing before him, I bared my soul, as well as the twenty-five pounds of pregnancy weight that I had gained so far (and not all in my belly, but mostly in my butt and hips) and asked him to accept everything, right then and there.

His eyes widened as he took in the rounded ball of belly that was our daughter. I watched expressions flicker across his face, expressions I couldn't quite decipher. What was he thinking? Was he happy? *He knows he's the father, right*? I couldn't deal with the silence. I needed to know how he felt.

"Surprise?" I said weakly. Shane finally let out his infectious laugh and helped me into my robe, then he wrapped his arms around me again. I exhaled. *So far so good.*

Shane rested his forehead on mine. "Extremely surprised. God, Megs, I've missed you so much."

Exhaustion poured off him and my soul ached. "You're here now. That's all that matters. Come on, let's sit."

We moved to the sofa in the family room. He pulled me into him and we sat in silence for a moment. The last time I saw Shane the FBI had stormed into our home and arrested him for possession of narcotics, distribution, and a whole rap sheet of other criminal charges that linked him to the Cruz Cartel, a large and dangerous drug ring. The man I saw in shackles in the FBI interrogation room was an entirely different Shane—a Shane that I had never known existed until that very day. Only a few people knew the truth: Shane dealt drugs for the Cruz Cartel in order to gain information to help the FBI. I only learned the truth when Tommy Greene, my ex-fiancé and the FBI agent handling Shane, explained it to me after Shane had been placed in protective custody. We thought he was safe. But he wasn't. The explosion that tore apart his safe house also tore a hole in my soul.

As elated as I was to have him back, seeing him here sent thousands of questions running through my mind. *How did he manage to survive?* And most importantly, what was going to happen now? I wrapped my arms around him.

"They told me you were dead. But I never gave up. I didn't want to believe it," I whispered. The thought of him dead, which had been a reality only a few short moments ago, brought a lump to my throat and clenched my heart.

"It was close. If I had been in another room, I wouldn't be standing here right now," he murmured.

I gazed into his eyes. "What happened?"

Shane sighed. A grimace crossed his face, a sure sign that he didn't want to talk about it. But I knew that once the world found out that he was alive, he would have to rehash everything all over again.

"Honestly, I'm not sure. I had just made a sandwich

when I heard shouting, then gunshots. Next thing I knew, there was a huge explosion. The blast threw me out of the glass door. I managed to crawl away and hide under a truck until it was safe enough to move. I waited there and watched the house burn down."

My heart stopped. He could have been killed, just like that. "How long were you underneath the truck?"

"About an hour or so. The house was pretty far away from any main street, so I waited until I heard sirens. Once I heard the sirens, I knew that whoever was still around would leave."

"Did the Cartel find you?" The expression on his face answered my question. I twisted my body to face him. "Shane, what happened when they found you?"

He shook his head. "Megan, it was bad. Please leave it at that. I managed to get away, but not without consequences. A lot went down that night. So much. I'm still trying to process it. I will tell you everything, I promise. I need you to know everything. But right now, I just want to be with you." Holding me close, he pressed his lips to my hair. I inhaled deeply, taking in the smell of old leather, dirt, and weariness. His body was fraught with tension and fatigue. My heart ached to see him this way.

"We don't have to talk about it now," I murmured into his chest.

Shane groaned and pulled me into his lap. "I know.

And it's late. I'm sure you're tired. I'm practically dead on my feet. I'm sorry I woke you up, but seeing you was my number one priority." He buried his head in my neck and squeezed me gently.

"Then let's go to bed," I whispered. The most important thing right now was that Shane was home and he was safe. The rest could wait until tomorrow. I got up from his lap and led him upstairs.

"Hey, Penny. Did you take care of our girl?" Shane said as he gave my dog, Penny, the ear massage that she loves. She closed her eyes blissfully and made a snuffling sound.

"Yes, she took care of your girls. Both of us," I corrected gently as I took out some of his clothes that I had stored.

Shane's mouth gaped open. "A girl? Really?" He took the clothes from my hands and tugged me into his arms. "She's going to be a handful, just like you. You know that, right?" he teased as his lips brushed mine.

I was lighter than air, but completely exhausted. I broke the kiss off with a yawn.

"Yes, a girl. I'll tell you all about her in a minute. But go get cleaned up so we can go to bed." I gently pushed him toward the bathroom. Shane gave me a tired grin.

"I haven't had a decent shower in ages." He kissed me lightly and headed into the bathroom.

I can't believe he's back. Shane was alive. But as

much as I wanted to be excited, my brain cautioned me otherwise. I'd had a feeling of dread ever since the night Tommy told me that Shane was instrumental in taking down the Cruz Cartel. Once the cartel realized my connection to Shane, the threat to our lives had become real. After I'd had the unfortunate experience of being at the end of a cartel member's fist, Tommy put my mother and me into hiding at his house in Deep Creek Lake in the hopes that the cartel wouldn't find me. But, somehow, they did, resulting in a car crash and a gunfight between the cartel and the FBI with me caught in the middle. I killed a man that night. The man was one of the leaders of the gang, and was the one who told me that Shane was dead. My life was spared, thanks to the heroic efforts of Kate Parker, Tommy's partner.

Tommy Greene. What would he think of Shane's return? Despite our history and his personal distaste for Shane, I was sure Tommy would be happy for me. He had helped me recover, both mentally and emotionally, after the incident at Deep Creek Lake. But Tommy was FBI, always had been and always would be. He would put the cartel business first and foremost. I was sure Tommy would sequester Shane, and separate us.

Last month, Tommy told me that the threat was still out there, that the cartel would be looking for revenge for the killings of two of their men. But because of the shake-up and the subsequent arrests made by the FBI and the

DEA, the cartel was running scared; I had become low on their list of priorities. *That will surely change once word gets out that Shane is back.* Lost in thought, I didn't know Shane had walked back into the room until he brushed my hair away from my shoulder.

"Baby? Are you okay?" he asked, his hazel eyes filled with concern. I smiled weakly.

"I'm shocked that you're still here. And to be honest, I'm waiting for you to disappear like you have all the other times," I said. Pent up emotion coursed through me and tears were running down my cheeks before I even realized they were there. Shane sat beside me, cradled my face with his large calloused hands, and stared into my eyes.

"I know, baby. I know. I'm here. And there is nothing in this world that will make me leave you again."

I tried to stay in control, but those words, his voice, his gaze caused every emotion to overwhelm me. Sobs racked my body. With tears streaming down my face, I felt his heartbeat next to mine as he held me tight. He stroked my back and whispered that he would always be here and that everything would be all right. As I started to calm down, hope took hold. *We will be fine.* Shane was home. I raised my head and stared into his beautiful hazel eyes. His anguish, heartache, and still-present passion shined brightly. I pulled him down to me and pressed my lips to his.

He kissed me back with everything he had, awakening my fervor that had been dormant for so long. His tongue caressed mine. His hands drew back my bathrobe and he wrapped his arms securely around me, pressing me as close to his chest as my belly would allow. I was dying inside; I needed him closer. I needed to touch him, to feel him, to have him touch me. It had been so long since we'd made love and, although I'd gotten some needed release with the help of my purple friend, I had craved Shane.

I raked my nails down his back and gently edged his gray boxers down around his hips. He groaned as my fingers traced the trail of hair down his stomach and then circled his thick cock. My pulse raced and I tilted my head back as his mouth grazed my neck. I was flying. His hands, so calloused and strong, made me feel so damn good. Then suddenly—I gasped in pain.

"What's wrong?" he asked, worried. "Did I hurt you? Did I hurt the baby?"

I sucked in a sharp breath. The baby had wedged her foot in my ribcage so hard that I could barely breathe. I nudged him away. "I need to stand up," I wheezed.

Shane gently drew me up as if I were made of glass. I pushed his hands away and massaged my side while I walked around the room.

"Megan? What's wrong? Are you okay?"

I giggled, but at the same time, I felt bad for him. He

didn't know all the quirks that came with pregnancy.

"Yeah, I'm fine. Little miss decided that my ribs would make for a great foot rest. Give me a minute; I'll work her down."

His concerned look faded into a beautiful smile. "See. I told you. Already giving you hell."

I grunted and continued to massage my side. That was pretty much the most effective cold shower I'd ever had. Nothing could kill the mood for sex like a baby kicking your butt from the inside. After getting comfortable again, I sat back down on the bed and leaned my head against Shane's shoulder.

"We really should get to bed," he whispered. I nodded, my eyes heavy with exhaustion. He smiled as he got up. He walked over to the bureau and pulled out his faded, red hockey practice shirt for me to sleep in, then he chuckled loudly.

"Since when did you start wearing granny panties?" Shane asked, holding up a pair of full coverage briefs.

"Since I became all about comfort. Besides, who's going to see me in my drawers? The doctor? I don't think I'm her type," I quipped as I snatched the offending pair out of his hands. Shane couldn't stop laughing as he helped me put them on. I rolled my eyes and climbed into bed. I didn't want to tell him that I had gained so much weight in my butt that the nice undies rode up. I was mortified as it was.

I rolled onto my side and scooted closer to him than I thought possible. As if he'd been doing it all along, Shane nestled up to me and wrapped his arm around my belly. Our daughter. For the first time in a long time, my heart filled with hope. I closed my eyes in disbelief and thanked the heavens.

"Your ass better be here when I wake up," I grumbled.

"Baby, I'm not going anywhere."

CHAPTER 2

"Don't fucking touch me!"

A shout pierced my subconscious and yanked me out of my blissful dream. Panicked, I sat up and looked around. Shane moaned and writhed in his sleep.

"Baby, it's okay. It's just a dream." I brushed the hair from my eyes and placed my hand on his chest. His body jerked as if I had stung him with an electric shock. He shot out of bed, falling into a defensive stance.

"Shane. It's me, Megan! You're home! Don't you remember?" I quickly asked as my heart pounded. I wanted to comfort him, to calm him down. Shane's eyes darted around the room as if looking for some kind of threat. Penny let out a low growl and jumped up on the bed, putting herself between Shane and me.

"Oh my God, Megan. I'm so sorry. I…I don't know what happened. Baby, I'm sorry," he apologized. His chest heaved with adrenaline and mortification filled his face. I played it off and laughed lightly to ease his concern.

"Hey, it's okay. I completely understand. You're not a morning person. I remember," I said nonchalantly. Beneath the bravado, I trembled inside.

Obviously taken aback by his outburst, Shane ran his hand through the mess on his head and frowned.

"No. It's not okay. I shouldn't have reacted like that." He came around to my side of the bed and folded me into his arms. My heartbeat calmed to a normal rhythm. I wrapped my arms around his waist; I could feel the tension in his coiled body.

"You can make it up to us by feeding us pancakes," I mumbled into his chest.

"Seriously. I'm sorry. I didn't mean to scare you," Shane said. He cupped my face and brought his lips to mine.

"I know. I'm fine. Really. It's not a big deal. After everything that's happened you're bound to have nightmares. It's okay," I replied. To show him I was telling the truth, and to gain a moment to think, I purposely let my cold hands wander underneath his gray boxers, causing him to yelp and jump.

"*Yeeaaaaaahhhh*! Okay! Okay! Pancakes it is!" Shane

cried. "Come on, Pen. Let's make some pancakes."

"Go! I'm starving. I'll be right down."

His eyes roamed my face to make sure I was being truthful. I gave him my best smile and that seemed to satisfy him. He whistled for Penny and headed downstairs.

I exhaled and reminded myself that Shane had been through hell and back over the last four months; he would need time to adjust to being home. *He will be fine. We will be fine. There is no need to be overly dramatic or to freak out.*

The smell of coffee brewing and bacon frying made my stomach growl, so I pulled on my sweats and padded down the stairs. Much to the chagrin of my OB / GYN, bacon had been a staple on my menu. I couldn't eat enough of it, and it sure as heck wasn't curbing the weight gain. The whole "eating for a healthy one" wasn't resonating with me; I ate for a damn army.

In my kitchen I found Penny patiently waiting by the stove where Shane was tackling a huge undertaking. Aside from the bacon, he had the bread toasted, the eggs fried and best of all, pancakes bubbling on the stove.

"Wow. Now this is a feast," I quipped, as I pulled out the orange juice and creamer from the fridge.

"I would've made some hash browns too, but you're out of potatoes. Is this okay? I mean; is there anything else you want?" he asked, as he flipped the pancakes.

My mouth watered when I saw blueberries in the batter.

"No, this is fine. The problem is I don't think there's enough for you," I joked. I poured myself a cup of coffee and sat down. Shane chuckled.

"I know enough never to fight a pregnant woman for food, but I have you beat on the appetite; I could eat a whole cow." He put some eggs and bacon into Penny's bowl, then dished out the food for us.

Our plates loaded, we dug in. After a few moments, all I could do was stare. Shane shoveled food into his mouth so quickly you'd have thought he'd been on a hunger strike for the past year. Watching him reminded me of Penny: scarfing up the food without even tasting it. Shane looked up long enough to see me watching him with my mouth open and smiled weakly.

"Sorry. It's been a while since I've had a good meal."

"No, it's fine. I should have fed you last night," I replied. "When was the last time you ate?"

Shane paused. "The last time I ate anything substantial was about four days ago in a diner. I guess I looked pathetic counting out change, so the waitress said dinner was on her."

"Where were you?" I asked, my head jumbled with questions.

"Outside of Memphis...I think," he mumbled with his mouth full of food. I gaped at him, my forkful of pancake momentarily forgotten.

"How did you get here? Did you walk?"

"I walked. I hitched rides with truckers. I took a couple of buses. I was lost for a while and ended up going in circles. It's hard to travel when you barely have any money and no ID." He stabbed his pancake forcefully. I could tell he was getting agitated, but the questions kept tumbling out.

"How did you get away from the house?" I asked quietly, knowing how uncomfortable the subject made him.

"Stole the agent's truck. Stole a couple, actually." Was it my imagination, or was there a dare in his tone of voice, as if he expected me to be mad or upset that he had to steal a car? Did he actually think I would give him crap about that?

"Well that's understandable. Did you…" I started to ask if he was able to get any sleep, but he quickly cut me off.

Shane sighed in frustration as he put his fork down. "Look. I'm sorry, but can we talk about something else? It's over and done with. Is it good enough to know that I'm here now and I'm alive?"

Uh, okay. It was a simple question and while I understood his strain on reliving those details, the reaction was not what I expected. I wanted to help him adjust to being out of danger and back home.

"Of course." I sipped my coffee. The tension

thickened and I had no idea how to salvage the morning. Luckily, my mother has impeccable timing. My cell phone rang loudly from its spot on the counter. The Bruce Springsteen ringtone let me know it was her. Shane glanced at me, startled.

"It's just Mom." I eased myself off the chair.

"Don't tell her I'm here. Please," he whispered urgently, his eyes wide.

I nodded and answered the phone. "Hi Mom, what's up?" I asked, keeping my voice light.

"Did you oversleep?" Mom asked. "We were wondering where you were." Confused for a moment, it suddenly dawned on me. I completely forgot about the post-wedding brunch for my brother, Kyle, and his new wife and my former college roommate, Sarah. *Oh crap.*

"I guess I did. I was exhausted last night. I'm sorry I missed it," I replied. I was genuinely apologetic. Brunch was at Uncle Bob's house on the Chesapeake Bay, as a way to say good-bye to Sarah and Kyle before they left on their honeymoon to St. Maarten.

"No worries. Brunch is over and there is still a ton of food. I'm sending Tommy over with some leftovers," she mentioned.

"Wait, what? Tommy's on his way here?"

"Yes, Megan. That's what I just said. He's on his way over with some crab cakes, scrambled eggs, fruit, those mini quiches you like, some bacon…Dear, try not to eat too much bacon, you know what the doctor said," my mom continued, unaware that her phone call set off an anxiety attack in Shane.

"Thanks, but that's not necessary. I'm not feeling so good; my stomach is kind of messed up. I think I ate too much last night," I rushed, suddenly nauseous. Shane's expression became thunderous. *What the heck just happened? Why is he so angry?* I gestured frantically for him to go upstairs and tried to listen to my mother prattle on.

"What Mom? Sorry, I'm a little distracted," I said, as Shane peered out the window.

"He's here," Shane whispered tersely.

"Mom, Tommy's here. I'm going to send him on his way. I really don't feel good." I quickly hung up in the middle of my mother's spiel. I've never done that before, but I pushed away the pang of regret and focused on Shane.

"Get him out of here Megan." Shane's terse order spoke volumes as he strode into the family room. He stood within eyesight of the mudroom door with his fists clenched, as if waiting for Tommy to come in with a shotgun. Granted, that's what happened the last time he was in my house; but that raid was just an act so that it would look like Shane was being arrested with the rest of the gang.

"Shane, Tommy is a good friend. It's okay," I

whispered.

"Just make him leave," he hissed. With my focus on Shane, Tommy's knock startled me.

I tightened my robe and opened the mud room door.

"Hey, Tommy. I'm sorry. I'm really not feeling well right now," I said weakly. Not feeling well was right on the money. Shane's behavior was making me dizzy.

"Babe, you don't look too good. Did you eat a lot of bacon again? You know what that does to you. Why don't I come in and make you a cup of tea." Tommy tried to gently nudge passed, but I blocked his way.

"I'm fine. I didn't eat a lot of bacon. I promise. I just have a really bad headache and I'm going back to bed." Again, not another lie. I could feel a migraine coming on.

He smiled and sniffed the air. "Yeah, sure you didn't eat a lot of bacon. I can smell it. But, it's cool. I need to head to Jersey for the day anyway. I'll be back tomorrow. Here's the bag from your mom. Do you need anything before I roll out?"

"No, I'm good. I'm just going to clean up, then go back to bed." I rubbed my head, gingerly.

"Well, I hope you feel better." He kissed my forehead. "Call me later if you need anything. I should be back around seven."

I nodded as he walked down the driveway and pulled away in his black Suburban. Shane came around the corner the moment I shut the door. His eyes were dark with fury and his face was pulled into a deep frown; he was furious. But I had no clue why.

"So, Tommy's been coming around here a lot, huh?"

"And what the hell is that supposed to mean?" I blurted out, taken aback by his question. *So much for my filter.*

Shane's eyes widened at my outburst then realization dawned on him; he knew he had screwed up.

"Shit. Nothing. I'm sorry. I really am. I'm just jealous. This is just really overwhelming." He drew me into his chest.

"I know." I closed my eyes at the thundering headache that loomed behind them.

"Why don't you go back to bed? I'll clean up here."

I accepted and padded up the stairs. But Shane's attitude really troubled me. I know he wants me to give him space, but he will have to let me in and let me help him. *We* will *talk about this, come hell or high water.*

***

AFTER MY NAP, I felt somewhat human. Tylenol and water sat on the nightstand next to me. Getting up and taking the pills, I slowly wandered down to the kitchen to find Shane at the table with my laptop. He was intently reading something, something that apparently was not for my viewing as he quickly closed the page when he saw me.

"Hey. How are you feeling?" he asked warily.

"Better. How about you?" I gave him a pointed look and he had the grace to look away. *Screw walking on eggshells, we're going to talk about what is going on.*

"Baby, I'm sorry for this morning. I really am. And I know I should be grateful that Tommy has been around to watch over you. But there is just something about him that bugs the hell out of me."

I wasn't sure how to take that. On one hand, he looked very remorseful and contrite. But on the other hand, the expression on his face when Tommy came to the door was murderous. Could he really believe that Tommy and I had a thing? I didn't say anything as I poured some water from the pitcher sitting on the table and sat across from him. Shane pushed aside the laptop and I took his hands.

"I know you're in a different place right now. Like you said earlier, this is very overwhelming. A lot has happened since you left. But the only way we're going to get through this is if we talk about it. I don't want you to hide anything from me or hold it back. We need to get it all out. I need you to talk to me." *Shit.* I meant to start off slow and gentle, but everything tumbled out. Shane closed his eyes and pinched the bridge of his nose, his telltale sign that he was trying to choose his words wisely.

"Megs, I'm not trying to hide anything from you. A lot of shit happened out there, and to be honest, it fucked me up more than I thought," he said carefully. I nodded, encouraging him to continue. He sighed and went on.

"The agent in charge at the safe house, Garrison, had been running on high alert all day. There was so much chatter coming in from their sources, everything from sightings of Reggie to locations of the heads of each group. There were even explicit details on where they were going to strike next. Garrison was going nuts, trying to decipher what was real and what was rumor. And then just like that, their radios went down. They couldn't check in with the field office or with other units. Garrison filled me in once they lost all communications."

"Did they know that the cartel was coming for you?" The brave façade I desperately tried to hold onto began to crumble. I wanted to be strong for him, to show him I could handle this, but the terror crept into my voice.

"Garrison knew something was up. It was no fluke that the radios and computers went dark. He wanted more agents on the ground, so they used their cell phones to call for backup. No one came and he was frustrated as hell. His gut was telling him to move, but his commands were to stay put. If we had followed Garrison's instincts, those agents would still be alive…"

he said sadly, his voice trailing off.

After a pause, he continued. "Anyway, we were trying to relieve the tension by playing video games. I went into the kitchen for a sandwich and that was it. After the explosion I told you about, I hid under the truck where I heard several cars come up the drive. I knew it was the cartel and I knew they were looking for me. I couldn't see much, just the shoes and rims of the tires. Megs, those were the same custom BCBG rims that Christian Cruz, the kingpin of the Cruz Cartel, required all his upper level guys to have. Then there were shots. Those bastards took out the four men that had stayed back at the house, men that died because of me. They were good guys, Megs, and I found them shot in the back."

I shuddered at the terror that he'd seen. But Shane couldn't stop. Once he started, the words flowed out like an avalanche.

"The cartel left as soon as they heard the sirens. I knew I had a limited time to get out. I broke Garrison's truck's window, hotwired the truck, and barreled out, like a bat out of hell. I drove for an hour before the cartel caught up with me. I was going so fast I lost control of the truck and crashed into a tree. They tied me up and blindfolded me, but I recognized some of their voices. I was thrown into a van and we drove for what felt like hours," he said in a rush, tripping over his words. Shane didn't add details, but he didn't have to. The tension in his jaw and his fixed stare at the table said it all. His fists clenched the placemat as he relayed what happened. Even though it had all happened months ago, it was clear that it was so very fresh in his memory. My heart ached for him.

"When we stopped, I was put into a dark room that was as small as your bathroom; it smelled as bad as my old hockey gear. There were two of them, big jacked-up guys, wearing ski masks watching over me and carrying AK-47s. They told me that Christian was on his way and that I would pay for ratting them out. The bastards kept me awake by watching their porn as loud as they could, or by bringing their dogs into the room. If they caught me dozing, I would get a bucket of cold water on my head or get dog shit thrown on me. They chained me to the wall and beat me with baseball bats, but only until I was on the verge of passing out. They fucked with my head. The biggest one giggled like a bitch every time."

I gasped. The thought of him being tortured and abused made my stomach turn. Shane kept his eyes down as the words continued to tumble out.

"I lost track of time, but I figured I was in there for a couple of weeks. They got piss drunk the day before Christian was supposed to show up. Stupid, piss-ass drunk. They had been fucking with me through the door and forgot to lock it after they brought me dinner, which was just a bunch of crap from the vending machine. They were so drunk they could hardly stand. I managed to get the chains off the wall, so I took a chance. I opened the door and beat the hell out of them with the chains. I shot them both with their own guns. I took what I could from their wallets and ran."

I gasped as my heart pounded. Shane's expression turned dark.

"Where were you? How did you manage to get home?"

Shane took a breath and continued with the story, anxious to get it out quickly. "I think we were in New Mexico or Arizona. It was hot as hell and there was a lot of desert. I caught a few rides with some truckers and somehow managed to get to the Kentucky-West Virginia border. From there I walked until an Iraq vet took pity on me outside of Charleston. That's who dropped me off last night."

I sat in awe as I listened to his journey.

"When I was stuck in that hellhole, I heard them talk about you and how Reggie had gone to find you." His voice tightened and he grabbed my hand. "It scared the shit out of me, to know that they had targeted you. That was the one thing I didn't want to happen. I thought I could protect you. But all I did was lead them right to you. If I hadn't moved back in…"

I had thought about the *ifs* too. *If* Shane hadn't been

dealing in the first place, *if* he hadn't gotten busted, *if* he hadn't made a deal with the Feds, none of this would have happened. But I didn't blame him. He had been only a teenager when his family died in a car accident. Alone and angry, he took refuge within a drug cartel, a drug cartel that called itself a family. But it was a family that wouldn't hesitate to slit your throat.

"I don't blame you. You couldn't have predicted this. There was nothing you could have done," I whispered, squeezing his hand.

"There was plenty I could have done early on to prevent this bullshit. But I was stupid then, and I'm paying the price now."

I sighed. There was no use arguing with him. He would always feel guilty.

"The fact that you're here now, that you risked everything, means the world to me. I can't imagine the horrors you faced." I had so much to say, but the words wouldn't form on my tongue. He smiled slightly.

"I never wanted to hurt you. It killed me when Tommy brought you to see me in jail. Seeing you cry is one hundred times worse than anything those assholes could have done to me," Shane whispered.

The memory of seeing him in jail came roaring back. The image of Shane in shackles made my stomach turn. I had said some pretty hateful things that day, and now I regretted every single one of them. I walked over to him and curled my arms around his shoulders.

"As much as I hated you in that moment, I still loved you. I have always loved you. And I have regretted that day ever since. The things I said—that was not the way I should have said good-bye." I brushed away the tears that had begun to stream down my cheek and gave him a shaky smile. "But you're here now and we have this opportunity to start over."

"I'm not going to screw this up again, Megs. I promise," he said with conviction, looking at me with hope-filled eyes.

"I know."

He heaved a sigh of relief and wrapped his arms around my waist, pulling me as close as the baby ball would allow.

The rest of the day passed more smoothly than the morning. We stayed in and finished up the leftover brunch snacks. I brought him up to speed on what had been going on with the cartel. With Reggie—Christian's cousin and the cartel's lead enforcer—gone and half of his crew arrested or dead, the Cruz Cartel was no longer a real threat. Tommy said that Christian was more concerned about his rivals gaining ground on their turf than with getting revenge. Shane listened carefully, absorbing all the information. He seemed devoid of emotion—until I told him what happened at Deep Creek Lake.

His jaw clenched and his hands curled into fists as I told him how Tommy, Kate, and I had made our escape until the cartel crashed into our SUV, causing a terrible gunfight in which Kate was shot while saving my life. Shane jumped up in rage, fury rolling off his body, as I whispered that I had shot and killed Reggie. He stalked around the room like a caged animal who was desperate to go after its prey.

"I knew something like this was going to happen. I fucking knew it. I swear, Megs. I will make them pay for what they did to you. I will slit their fucking throats," he growled. The vengeance in his voice made me flinch. Even though it gave me sort of a thrill to hear that he loved me enough to want to avenge the horror I'd endured, the knowledge that he was capable of it terrified me.

"Look. It's over now. I'm fine. We're safe." I stood and wrapped my arms around his waist. He closed his eyes and cradled my head in his huge, calloused hands.

"I know. But I can't help it. You're the most important thing in my life. The fact that I wasn't there to protect you breaks me. I did a fucked-up job protecting you before, I'm not going to let that happen again," he said with resolve. Not knowing what else to say, I hugged him tighter and prayed he wouldn't have to try.

CHAPTER 3

THE NEXT MORNING I woke to sunlight on my face. I rolled over and looked at the man lying face down beside me. My lustful gaze trailed up from the small of his back, past the colorful dragons and serpents etched onto his ribs and spine, to the sexy rigid muscles in his upper back. I wanted to touch him, to let him know I was here, but I remembered his hair-trigger response the day before and decided against it.

Not a day had gone by that I hadn't dreamed about Shane and that one day he would come home to us. I imagined that our days would be filled with long talks and moments of reconnection, and our nights would be full of hot, sweaty sex. But things weren't going the way I had imagined. *Baby steps, Megan. He just needs to adjust.*

I couldn't change the past and we would have to take things in stride. We couldn't be the same couple we once were, not overnight.

I got up, shrugged on my bathrobe and shuffled downstairs. I called Uncle Bob at the law office where I worked to remind him that I had a doctor's appointment that afternoon and that I had decided to take the entire day off. Right away Bob assumed the worst. I quickly reassured him that it was purely a routine checkup and that I was feeling fine. After calming his nerves, I hung up the phone and felt a pang of guilt for not telling him about Shane. Uncle Bob had been instrumental in negotiation the plea agreement with the FBI that got Shane into protective custody. He thought of Shane as his son and was completely devastated when we learned that Shane's safe house had been bombed. I brushed aside the guilt and pulled out a carton of eggs and some fruit from the fridge. It would only be a matter of time before everyone learned that Shane was back, so for moment I heeded his request to keep his homecoming a secret.

I had just let Penny outside and cracked the eggs into the pan when Shane sauntered into the kitchen. I glanced over my shoulder and let out a soft gasp. His brown hair glistened from the shower, curling around his studded ears. Gray sweatpants hung low on his hips. His wire-rimmed glasses looked out of place on a man with tribal symbols and dragons inked over his sculpted chest and abs. The man was pure sex, no doubt about it. My voiced hitched as I managed to say, "Good morning, baby."

"Good morning," he said, his voice still thick with sleep. He wrapped his muscular arms around my belly from behind me, the evidence of his arousal pressed against the small of my back. My breath caught and my heart quickened as he nuzzled the sensitive spot under my ear. Just this one simple act had my core pulsing with liquid heat. His hands roamed north, barely grazing my belly, and tenderly kneaded my swollen breasts. Moaning, I tilted my head up toward his and caught his searing lips with mine.

Abandoning the pan in front of me, I turned and threw my arms around his neck. Passion fueled my body as our lips frantically mashed together. Our tongues clashed, dueling over the right to invade the other's mouth. Shane's hands cupped my behind, then gripped hard as he led me over to the table. He swept aside the napkins and papers that covered it and lifted me onto the smooth surface.

Red colored my vision as my primal need took over. Shane pulled off my bathrobe at the same moment I yanked down his sweatpants. My mouth watered at the size of his erection and I eagerly stroked his throbbing, rigid shaft. His head rolled back and he groaned at my touch. There was a time for cuddling and foreplay, but this wasn't it. His hazel eyes smoldered, and he desperately ripped the thin material of my cotton underwear right out from under me. Craving his touch, his body, his heat against mine, I leaned back on my elbows and gave him the opening he wanted.

Without hesitation, Shane plunged his engorged cock into me. I was ready for him and gasped a ragged breath as he slid against my inner walls. My body clearly remembered his, anticipating each plunge and pull. He angled his hips, hitting the right spot with each thrust, and leaned forward to gently nibble the hollow of my neck. My thighs wrapped around him, clenching him to me as he gripped my hips. He let out a guttural groan and buried his cock so deep inside me he filled me more than I'd ever been filled before. I reached up and clung to his shoulders, hanging on as I exploded.

With a final jerk, Shane's body went limp and his legs trembled slightly. He brushed his lips against my jawline and murmured, "I love you so much."

I was about to respond when I smelled something in the air. *What the hell? Is something burning?* I glanced over his shoulder and saw smoke rising off the pan.

"Oh shit, the eggs!" I cried, untangling my legs from around his waist. Shane laughed and pulled up his pants. He walked the five feet to the stove and turned off the burner. Steam filled the air and the pan sizzled when he tossed it into the sink full of water.

"I hope you weren't craving eggs," he joked, as he helped me down from the table.

"Nope. I'm feeling pretty satisfied right now," I replied with a smile.

Shane smirked, and then a worried look came over his face. "I didn't hurt you, did I? I mean, the baby..."

"No, the baby's fine. In fact, she's moving around now. Here, feel her," I said gently, putting his hand on our daughter's thumping rump. His eyes grew wide as he felt her kick for the first time.

"That's so damn cool." The smile he gave me would be one that I knew I would remember my entire life.

"Yes, it is. Until she's sitting on my bladder or kicking the crap out of my windpipe," I quipped. I reached up and smooched him on the lips. "And I love you, too." Shane wrapped his arms around me in a tight hug.

We stood there, basking in the aftermath of our table session. All the worry and negative thoughts were gone, and for a moment, I had a fleeting fantasy that our lives were back to normal. Reality came crashing down, though, when he reluctantly released me.

"What's on tap for today?" He asked, returning our conversation back to the present and pouring himself some coffee.

A little jumbled from my fall from euphoria, I shook the cobwebs out of my brain. The reintroduction to amazing sex had messed with my head.

"I have a doctor's appointment at one, if you'd like to come," I offered, but knowing his need for solitude, I didn't press the suggestion.

Shane shook his head. "I would love to, but I'm not too crazy for public places right now. Especially when I don't know what's going on with Reggie's crew." I knew it would be futile to try to reassure him, so I nodded my acceptance.

Sensing my disappointment, he tried to apologize, but I cut him off. "It's okay. I totally understand. I'm not upset. I'll record the appointment, so it will be like you were there. Besides, I have to take a glucose test, so there's no point in you sitting around with me for an hour." I didn't want him to feel pressured into venturing out when he was not ready. "What are you going to do?"

"I'm not sure yet. I was thinking about going into the shed and tinkering with the bike. Wait, is the bike still in there? And where's my truck?"

I burst out laughing at his concern. "Adrian, like the great friend he is, has been taking wonderful care of it. It wasn't doing me any good since I can't get my preggo self into the cab. And your bike is in the shed, awaiting your return. I couldn't bear to part with it."

Relief that his pride and joy was still around was evident in his face. I smiled as I poured two bowls of cereal and handed one to Shane. We sat at the table and idly chatted about how well the Baltimore Ravens had been doing. But despite the casual and light conversation, I knew he wasn't fully engaged. His leg jiggled in trepidation and his gaze darted between both entryways, as if he was waiting for the signal to run. It was all I could do not to hold him and tell him that we were fine.

Having him home was my dream come true. It was a freaking miracle. But it was also a constant reminder of the hell we had gone through and the danger that might still be ahead. I had the uneasy feeling that something was going to happen, and that a nervous and skittish Shane was the best I could hope for. I prayed for all of our sakes, that feeling was wrong.

CHAPTER 4

I LEFT SHANE WATCHING ESPN and went upstairs to get ready. While drying off from my shower, I contemplated how to ease Shane back into public life. We could only avoid my mother and brother for so long, and soon the holidays would be here. *How long can this go on?* Penny's sharp bark and a shout from downstairs caused me to jump and almost slip on the wet floor. *What the hell is going on?* I quickly threw on my robe and hustled down the stairs.

I watched in horror as Shane and Tommy wrestled on the ground, pummeling each other. "What the fuck is going on? Stop it right now! What the hell, Tommy? Why are you here?"

Breathing heavily, Tommy stood up. A drop of blood

trickled out of his nose. "Making sure you're not dead on the floor, Megan. I went by your office and you weren't there."

Shane, unscathed and furious, snorted. "So that gives you the right to just walk in?"

"Megan didn't show up for work, her phone went straight to voicemail, and no one answered the door. What the hell would you think? I have a key so I can make sure she's okay," Tommy said with disgust. He straightened his suit jacket and gave me the raised eyebrow. "I see you're okay."

I closed the gap in my robe and stood closer to Shane. "Yeah, I'm fine. I was in the shower. I didn't realize you were looking for me."

Shane scoffed. "You don't have to explain yourself to him." I shot him a look and quickly jabbed him in the ribs with my elbow. "What? You don't!"

"Shane, stop. As you can see, Tommy, everything's fine."

Tommy shook his head. "No shit. I can see that now. Imagine my surprise when I walk in and get punched in the face by a ghost. I thought you were dead, man."

The look he gave Shane was hard to read. Was Tommy happy to see Shane alive? Shane's body tightened and his eyes blazed. "Obviously the motherfuckers failed."

"Thank you, Captain Obvious. What the hell happened out there? Don't get me wrong; I'm glad you're alive. But we searched that area inch by inch. Bodies were everywhere. How the fuck did you escape?"

Shane's eye twitched and he clenched his fist. Fearing another explosion, I immediately stood between them.

"Do we have to do this? Shane just got home. Let's not do an extensive interrogation right now. Please, Tommy," I said in a low voice. The last thing I needed was for Shane to go Rambo-style crazy on Tommy for asking questions that he wasn't ready to answer.

"I can't just let this go. We need to bring him in for questioning. Agents died out there. They died protecting him. We need to know what happened and what he saw."

"And you'll get your chance. Just not right now. If he goes with you, then who the hell knows when I'll see him again." I stood firm, raising my chin to meet Tommy's glaring green eyes.

Tommy threw up his hands with a growl. "You have until eight tomorrow morning. Not one minute longer. I mean it, Megan. Shane better be at the office no later than eight. One minute later and I'm putting out a warrant for his arrest."

He brushed past us, knocking his shoulder into Shane as he stalked out of the kitchen door. Shane scowled at Tommy's retreating figure, his fists clenched and ready to drop Tommy to the floor. I quickly shut the door and gently pushed Shane back.

"Well, that was exciting," I quipped nervously. I shuffled through the kitchen and into the living room and was headed toward the stairs when Shane's voice stopped me.

"Why does he have a key, Megan? Is there something I need to know?"

Incredulously, I whipped around to face him. "Really? We're going to go through this again? Fine, let's do this. He's my friend, Shane. He's been here for me for the last four months while I was going through hell. Gee, why was I going through hell? Because some deranged drug cartel was hunting me down. Because I killed a man in self-defense. Because everyone said you were dead and I couldn't imagine going on without you. That's why he has a key. He saved our lives, Shane, more times than I care to count."

"And he's also your ex-fiancé. He loved you once. Shit, probably still loves you. I'm sure that bastard thought nothing about moving right into my place."

"And what? You think that I gave up on you that easily? That the death of my soul mate was so easy to get over that I hopped in bed with the first man who didn't want to kill me? Are you fucking kidding me right now? Do you hear the bullshit that is coming of your mouth?" Disbelief surpassed the overwhelming rage that was flowing through my veins. *Seriously? Is this really happening?*

I cut him off as soon as he opened his mouth. "I have to get going. We'll talk about this more when I get back." I hurried up the stairs, leaving him to stew in my anger.

I fumed and went over every bit of the conversation while I dried my long dark-brown hair. *Is this going to happen every time Tommy comes over? Is Shane going to think there is some ulterior motive?* Briefly, my mind flitted back to two months ago, when I felt the baby kick for the first time. Tommy's words, his plea to be the baby's daddy and his promise that he would take care of us forever, echoed in my ears. There was no way I would tell Shane about that. There was no point. I had made my feelings abundantly clear to Tommy that day when I told him bluntly that Shane would always be my child's daddy and that no one would ever take his place.

After searching through clothes that couldn't accommodate my ever-growing belly, I finally settled on a pair of maternity jeans and a brown long-sleeved T-shirt. I slipped on my brown flats and walked down toward the kitchen. I stopped when I saw Shane waiting for me at the bottom of the stairs.

"I keep screwing this up. I'm sorry. I really am. I don't like Tommy. I don't trust the bastard, especially after all the shit that's gone down. Call it jealousy, call it a pissing match, call it whatever. It bothers the heck out of me that he was here for you when I wasn't. And it kills me that you almost married that douche."

Shane took my hand, leading me down the last two steps. He wrapped his arms around my waist and pressed his lips to my forehead. I sighed, my eyes closed tightly. I wanted to understand, to let this little incident gloss over. But his mistrust hurt way too much.

"Okay," I whispered, my voice strained. Suddenly exhaustion came over me. The stress from the day's events was overwhelming me. I needed time to think, to distance myself from the drama. *The shit hasn't even hit the fan yet and I'm already done with it.* The firestorm that was potentially brewing gave me heartburn, and not the normal pregnancy-induced kind.

"Megs…" Shane started.

I gently slipped out of his arms. "I have to get going. I have to…deal with this my own way. But please understand this: as much as I love you, as much as I have your back and will do anything I can for you, I can't just push Tommy away now that you're home. Tommy is my friend, nothing more, and he will remain so. You're going to have to try to tolerate him. I'm not asking for a BFF bromance, just tolerance." I lightly pecked his cheek. "I'll be back in a couple of hours."

He nodded, his expression twisted in guilt. Grabbing my purse and jacket from the mudroom, I hurried out of the door to my car and wiped away the tears of frustration as I drove away.

CHAPTER 5

ONCE I ARRIVED AT THE medical center, the attending nurse took my vitals and then sent me to the lab to drink the vile, disgustingly sweet concoction that would test my blood sugar for pregnancy-induced diabetes. With an hour to wait before my appointment, I sat in the waiting room while the last couple of days surfaced in my mind. Shane had definitely changed into someone I didn't completely recognize. Granted, we had both been through a difficult time, but his attitude and demeanor baffled me. Had he always been this insecure? Did he really think I would be with Tommy?

The thoughts collided in my head. Doubt and fears overwhelmed me as I worked myself into a frenzy. Would we make it? Would he be able to come to grips with everything that had happened?

April, the attending nurse, called my name and startled me from my thoughts. As she got me settled onto the paper-covered table, Dr. DeVaughn walked in. She took one look at me and said, "Is everything okay? You don't look so good."

What could I say? That my boyfriend was back from the dead, acting terribly strange, and stressing the hell out of me? No, not quite. I mumbled something about traffic and received the standard lecture about limiting my stress and resting my body and brain.

"Unfortunately, your test results aren't looking too promising. With the weight you've gained and the results measuring high, I think it's best to put you on a lower carbohydrate diet," she explained patiently.

My eyebrows shot to my hairline and my mouth gaped open. "What does that mean, exactly?"

Dr. DeVaughn gave me the no bullshit look my mom normally gives me when I ask stupid questions. "It means that in order to keep yourself and your daughter healthy, you need to cut back on the junk food. It means more protein and less sugar." She handed me a pamphlet.

"So there goes any chance of getting a Frosty and fries later on," I grumbled.

Dr. DeVaughn gave me a sidelong look, then asked me to lay back. She squirted the warm, green jelly over my belly and set the Doppler on the most protruding part. This was my favorite part of the exam. Apparently, Little Miss didn't appreciate the pressure and immediately started to move around. Dr. DeVaughn and I laughed. Even with this break in tension, I still felt sad. Shane should have been witnessed this. While I understand that he had no choice but to miss the last sonogram, now that he was home I wanted him to be a part of this. Being a part of the pregnancy of his first child was a once in a lifetime opportunity and he was missing it.

I quickly pressed the video record button on my phone and held it up to the monitor as the sound of my daughter's heartbeat filled the room. The galloping thumping always brought tears of joy to my eyes and today was no exception.

Twenty minutes later, I walked out with a pamphlet on gestational diabetes, a grumpy attitude, and a bruise from where the tech had drawn my blood. *The fun times when I could gorge on pizza and ice cream have come to a screeching halt.* Of course, the moment I was told I couldn't have carbs was the moment my cravings really kicked in. The thought of a big bowl of Mama Lucia's famous spaghetti and meatballs made my mouth water.

So I did what any hungry pregnant woman would do; I headed to the store. With Shane back, eating me out of house and home, I needed to stock up on more than just cereal and frozen dinners. As I waited at the light to cross over to Wegmans, I mentally went through the grocery list.

BAM.

The sound of crunching metal and squealing brakes filled my ears as my body flew forward, my belly slamming into the steering wheel on impact only to be immediately jerked back by the seatbelt. Then another hit from the side. My head connected with the side airbag and stars danced in front of my eyes. The pain in my shoulder screamed down my chest and into my stomach. Gasping for breath, I looked around. I had been hit so hard my car was sitting in the middle of Route 3. People were out of their cars, examining the scene before them. A man with dark-brown hair stood at my door, telling me to unlock it. With shaking hands, I pressed the unlock button. The man jerked it open.

"Ma'am, are you okay? Can you move?" he shouted. Why is he shouting? I wondered vaguely as I tried to nod. I grimaced as another pain shot through me.

"The ambulance is already on its way. Don't worry, I'm here to help. Try to remain still. Does anything hurt?"

Panic surged through me. "My ba...ba...baby," I stuttered. Disoriented and confused, I struggled to get the seatbelt off only to have the man rush to stop me.

"Ma'am, you need to stay still. Help is coming. I

want you to talk to me until they get here." His voice, tinged with a hint of a Baltimore accent, was calm and collected. I managed to nod as my eyes wandered over to the carnage in front of me. Twisted metal and shattered glass was everywhere. *Oh my God! Is that blood on my hood?* The world came rushing back as I began to comprehend the scene before me. Suddenly the screams wouldn't stop.

The brown-eyed man winced at my screaming and gently held my hand. "No, no, ma'am. Stay focused on me. What's your name?"

I had just opened my mouth to answer when I heard a shout from outside the car.

"Megan? Holy shit, Megan!" A voice boomed from behind the man with the brown eyes. Adrian Michaels, Shane's best friend, ran toward the car. "I was driving by and recognized your car. Are you okay? What happened?"

"Adrian! Oh my God, Adrian! Adrian!" I screamed. Trembling violently, I grabbed his hand. The mystery man muttered something about shock and possible head injury.

"You're going to be okay, Megs. I promise. You're going to be fine."

Finally, the ambulance and police pulled up to the scene. The EMTs secured a brace around my neck and, with the mystery man's help, slid me onto a backboard.

Adrian walked along with me and told me that he'd call my mom to meet me at the hospital. *Shit. She's going to have a heart attack.* But there was only one person I needed by my side.

"No. Not Mom. Shane."

Adrian's chiseled face shifted into a worried frown. He obviously thought I had hit my head harder than previously thought. "Megs, let me call your mom."

"No, dammit. Get Shane. Go to my house and get Shane!" I managed to get out. He gave me a placating look that made me want to jump off the damn gurney and smack him upside the head. *Don't fucking stand there, just do it!*

The EMTs slammed the ambulance doors shut, and we sped toward the hospital with sirens blaring. They started an IV and checked my vitals before I even realized what had happened. I quickly took stock of my situation. The baby was moving and my stomach was cramping ever so slightly. My shoulder and neck were in pain, but nothing felt broken. I closed my eyes and prayed that nothing was wrong with the baby. I could live with a busted shoulder, but not without my baby.

Within minutes the ambulance pulled up to the very hospital center I had just left. As the EMTs hustled me into the chaotic ER, I heard a familiar voice across the hall.

"What the hell did you do now?" My best friend,

Jennifer Walsh, was on duty as the head trauma nurse. *Thank goodness. A friendly face.* She took the gurney from the EMTs and wheeled me to a room. I snorted as tears ran down my face.

"Oh, you know me. I can't be me without some sort of drama," I remarked sarcastically as I broke down in tears. Jen hurriedly closed the curtain around my slice of privacy and quickly came over to the gurney to give me a gentle embrace.

"You're going to be fine. Let's just see how baby Katie is doing, shall we?" she said calmly as she wrapped an elastic band over my belly. After Jen adjusted the monitors, Katie's rhythmic heartbeat came through loud and clear. Jen then retook my vitals and asked me a few questions. She was in her element, her domain, and she was in control. I felt relief that she was there and my anxiety lessened slightly.

"Dr. DeVaughn is coming down now and will examine you before we get you into CT and X-ray. Does anything hurt? Do you want me to call your mom?"

I hesitated. *Well heck, the world is going to know sooner or later.* Thankfully, Dr. DeVaughn pulled back the curtain.

"Wasn't expecting to see you so soon, Megan. How are we doing?" she asked, her no-nonsense voice gentler and kinder than normal. After looking at the fetal monitor printout, she turned back to me. "Are you feeling any pain? Any cramping?"

Shivering with fear, I nodded. "My back is killing me. Is the baby all right?"

Dr. DeVaughn frowned. "Well, that's to be expected. You're going to be sore for a while." She palpated my abdomen and nodded. "Good. Nice and soft. I'm not seeing anything to suggest that something is wrong with the baby. There are some mild contractions on the monitor, but it's nothing to worry about. We'll give you some medication to stop them and keep you overnight for observation. Dr. Tio is the on-call doctor tonight, so she'll keep an eye on you when I'm not here." While Dr. DeVaughn was finishing my exam, a young female attendant coughed behind the curtain and stepped forward.

"Hi, Ms. Connors. I'll be taking you to CT." The young woman turned to Dr. DeVaughn and said, "Her husband is here to see her. Should I bring him back?"

Dr. DeVaughn knew my current marital status. She turned to me and asked, "Husband?"

I nodded quickly; my need for Shane to be with me was greater than any secret. Jen gaped at me. Her mouth dropped in shock as Shane parted the curtain and stepped inside. Dressed in jeans and a hooded sweatshirt, he looked almost exactly the same way he had when Jen saw him last. She paled as a slight gasp escaped her.

"How the hell—? I mean…You're…you're…alive? Oh my God! You're alive!" she shrieked, jumping into his arms. Shane wrapped his arms tightly around the woman he loved as a sister, all the while fixing his eyes on me.

"I'll explain it all later, okay, Jen?" Releasing her, he came over to my side and gently cupped my face in his large, calloused hands. "How are you doing?"

"Better now that you're here," I whispered, holding his hand against my cheek.

"I'm staying with you. I'm not leaving your side ever again," he muttered softly.

Dr. DeVaughn coughed and turned to the intern. "She's ready for CT now." She squeezed my shoulder. "I'll be back soon."

I closed my eyes tightly as tears escaped down my cheek. Knowing I wasn't going to be alone made me feel a little relieved, but I was desperate to know more about the baby. Shane's body suddenly tensed when we heard a commotion outside the curtain. His hands clenched, ready to protect us. But once he heard my mother's voice, his face softened into a smirk and he chuckled wearily.

"What the hell do you mean, 'Her husband is with her'? I think I would know for damn certain if my daughter was married. Now step aside right now before I throw you out of my way. My daughter needs me."

My mom swept the curtain aside and stepped into the room. She immediately sought out my eyes with hers, then stared directly at Shane.

"What the—? Shane?" she said, taking a step forward. Then she fainted.

I covered my face with my hands and shook my head. "Oh, fuck."

CHAPTER 6

A<small>FTER MY MOM HAD COME TO</small> with the help of some smelling salts and Dr. DeVaughn had checked her over, the interns wheeled me down the hall to radiology for a CT scan of my head and an X-ray of my back. Once they made sure that I did, in fact, still have a brain and that nothing was wrong with it, they took me to the maternity ward. The lusty cries of newborns and jovial male voices filled the air. *As long as the baby keeps cooking, that'll be us in a few months!* I thought, wiping away tears of anticipation.

The adrenaline and shock had worn off and the day's events cascaded over me like a waterfall. Exhausted and sore, I wanted nothing more than to sleep in my own bed. As the nurses assisted me in getting on to the hard-as-a-rock hospital bed, I looked around for Shane and my mom. Dr. DeVaughn saw the question on my face.

"They'll be right up. We sent them to the cafeteria with Jennifer. I'm not sure what was going on, but things looked tense, and you don't need that right now. We need to keep you relaxed," Dr. DeVaughn said.

To say the situation was tense was an understatement. At the moment, anything could be detrimental to Shane's sense of stability, from too much isolation to too much excitement. After this morning, who the heck knows how he'd react. Dr. DeVaughn explained to me how the next twenty-four hours would go and said that hopefully I'd be discharged the next day. With a gentle pat on the hand, she made her exit. The nurse, Melanie, showed me how the TV remote worked, how to position the bed, and the location of the button to call them if I needed anything.

After tucking the blankets around my legs, she shut the door behind her and left me in peace. Reclining the bed into a more comfortable position, I clicked on the TV and looked for something more substantial to watch than a *Jerry Springer* rerun. I settled on an *I Love Lucy* episode but watched with little interest, paying more attention to the sounds outside the door as I anticipated Shane's return. *Maybe he got lost. Maybe Tommy picked him up for his interview.* My thoughts were vague and scrambled. I felt the prick of a headache coming on, and

I closed my eyes to relieve it.

The sound of crinkling newspaper caused me to open up my eyes. Momentarily confused, I lifted my hand toward my forehead and felt the dull ache where the IV was shoved into my vein. The memories flooded back. I turned my head and Shane's face came into view.

"Hey, baby. How are you feeling?" he asked, his voice husky with concern.

I wetted my parched lips. "Okay, I think. Sore. How long have I been asleep?"

"About three hours. We came in and you were sound asleep. Your mom just walked downstairs to call your brother. She won't leave without seeing you."

I took a long draw of the water he offered and handed it back. "How did it go with Mom while I was getting my head examined?"

He snorted. "Better than expected. As soon as she was upright, she smacked me upside the head for making her faint. Then she smacked me again for making you two worried. But then she gave me a hug and told me that she was glad to see me."

I smiled as I imagined my five-foot-six-inch mother belting six-foot-two-inch Shane. It wasn't the first time she'd smacked him upside his head and probably wouldn't be the last. "What about Jen?"

"Jen was cool. We talked about what went down. I didn't go into detail about what happened; I just gave her a brief, less-dark overview. But don't worry about that. What did the doc say?"

"She said everything looks fine and as long as the contractions stop, I can go home tomorrow."

Shane nodded. "That's what they told me too. Um, I hope you didn't mind that I told them I was your husband. That was the only way I could think of to get them to let me in."

"We've been through hell and back. Plus, you knocked me up. I think that makes us practically married," I joked. Shane's expression suddenly changed and he looked down at the floor. My heart sank a little, but I quickly changed the subject. "I'm glad Adrian managed to find you. I'm sure it was a huge shock for him to see you."

Shane's face broke into a smile. "Yeah, I was in the shed and popped my head out when he pulled into the driveway. I swear he was going to pass out. It took him a full minute to realize I was alive, and then it was as if I'd never left. He's going to drop by in a couple days so we can catch up." Shane's expression grew dark. "But maybe I shouldn't be around. I'm back for a couple of days and already you're hurting."

Oh shit, not this. Not now. "That's baloney. It was an accident. It had nothing to do with you."

"It just seems suspicious, that's all. I mean, hell Megs, you could have died. Your car's totaled."

"I haven't seen the police report, but I'm sure whoever hit me is going to be charged with something. Accidents happen, Shane. This is all a coincidence," I replied confidently. However, the little voice in my head wondered the exact same thing Shane did. *Could this be the cartel? Are we about to go through all that drama all over again?*

"We'll see what the police report says. If they don't charge the bastard, we're going to have a face-to-fist meeting," he glowered.

I grabbed his hand and tried to lessen his anxiety. "Look, I'm fine. The baby is fine. And I was thinking about getting a new car anyway. Now the choice is made for me."

Shane gave me a tight smile and squeezed my fingers gently. "Maybe you're right. Just think, now you can get a minivan."

"I am never driving a mommy mobile. I don't care how many kids we have. I have an image to uphold," I quipped, fighting back the gnawing fear that was lodged in my stomach. I didn't want Shane to overreact, so I didn't tell him that the feeling of doom had never gone away despite Tommy's assurances that I was low on the cartel's priority list.

We heard a knock on the door, and then my mother's face popped through the privacy curtain.

"Oh, baby girl. I'm so happy that you're okay. How

are you feeling? Are you in pain? Are you hungry? How's my granddaughter doing?" she questioned, her fingers brushing my hair off my forehead.

"Hey, Mom. I'm stiff as hell. The baby is fine. We should be able to go home tomorrow," I replied, enjoying the feeling of her warm hands on my face.

"I'm glad you're awake. I needed to see for myself that you're all right. And now that Shane's here, I know you're in good hands. I'll run to your place and grab a few things. Do you want some dinner? The doctor said you could have something light, so I can bring you back some chicken soup."

"That sounds perfect. Thank you." She kissed my forehead and wiped away a tear, then grinned.

"Maybe I should drop off the blue box as well," she joked.

"No, Mom," I warned. Shane's eyes darted between the two of us as I gave my mom a pointed look.

"What's in the blue box?" he asked.

"Nothing. Don't worry about it. It's an inside joke," I said, shooting a laser-like glare at my mother who had the audacity to chuckle.

"Uh…okay. You know what? I think I'll catch a ride home with your mom. That way she doesn't have to make a trip back and I can grab the truck. Adrian had Ryan bring it to the house. Do you want anything in particular?"

"Just socks. My feet are freezing. Be safe out there."

Shane brought my purse over to the side table so I could use my phone. He brushed his lips against mine and quickly followed my mother out the door.

After I called Uncle Bob to let him know the latest, I watched soap opera reruns while waiting for Shane to return. Just as the nurse was finishing up one of her many checkups, Tommy walked in holding a vase filled with beautiful flowers.

"Hey there. How're you doing?" he asked, setting the vase down and kissing my cheek. Tommy shrugged off his black suit jacket and laid it across the back of Shane's vacated chair before sitting down. He ran his hand through his short blond hair. His green eyes were filled with concern.

"Hey. We're fine. Just some bumps and bruises."

"Good to hear. Your mom called me after she spoke with Jen. I got over here as fast as I could."

So that's how he found out. "You just missed her and Shane. Shane will be back shortly," I replied, hoping that he'd get the message and bug out before Shane returned. I didn't need another WWE-type brawl.

He smirked. "I don't doubt that. No worries, I'm not here for a rematch. I'm just checking in on you."

"Thanks. I appreciate it. Knowing you, you probably looked at the police reports. Do you know what they say?"

"Yeah, I spoke with the lead officer on the case. The guy, Gregory Sweeney, was charged with reckless endangerment, negligence, and a whole host of other traffic violations. His brakes were totally gone. That's why he hit you; he couldn't come to a complete stop. Aside from a few DUI's, the guy is clean. The driver coming from the opposite direction was Mitchell Torres, a sixty-five-year-old. He's in for observation, but the docs say he should be released in a day or so. This could have been a whole lot worse. The carnage of the vehicles tells a different story. All three are totaled."

Knowing the crash wasn't intentional relieved some of my stress. "So, this was purely an accident, right?"

Tommy raised his eyebrow. "Yeah. Just an accident. Why would you think otherwise?"

"It's stupid, but Shane was worried that the cartel was coming after me again."

Tommy shook his head. "I haven't seen the slightest inkling that the cartel is back in town. They're probably in Florida; there's a lot of noise down there right now, a lot of infighting between the leaders. Everything is up in the air. Our informant says that other cartels have picked up on the miscommunications within the group and are using it to their advantage. You're nonexistent on their radar right now, babe."

If there was ever a time that being invisible was a good thing, this was it. "What about now that Shane's back? He knows too much. Won't that up the ante?"

"Doubtful. Again, there's too much drama in the cartel right now, too much distrust and animosity between the leaders. Going after Shane isn't worth the risk or exposure. Remember, everything that went down over the summer is old news. New cartels and gangs are encroaching on the Cruz's territory. They are more worried about that than Shane."

"As long as you're sure."

"Trust me, Megs. I want to bring these guys down as much as anyone else, but I sure as hell won't risk your lives to do it. After Shane's meeting tomorrow, that's it. You guys are done with the situation. And I'll be on the lookout for anything suspicious."

"Thanks, Tommy," I said softly just as his phone beeped. He checked the message and swore under his breath. "What's wrong?" I asked.

Tommy grinned sheepishly. "I'm late. I am supposed to meet Jessica in ten minutes."

His boyish smile made me curious. "And who is Jessica?" I teased.

"I met her at the shooting range last week. She's cool."

Is that "guy speak" for hot as hell? I wondered and laughed at his nervousness. "It's rude to keep her waiting. Besides, Shane will be here soon and I don't want him to give you a black eye to go with your fat lip right before your date," Tommy scoffed and then leaned over and kissed me on my cheek again.

"I'm glad you're okay. I'll talk to you tomorrow," he said just before turning and bumping right into Shane's hard chest.

"Tommy," was Shane's only response to the physical contact.

"Shane," Tommy replied with a nod. He turned, winked at me, and said "Later Megs." He left, closing the door behind him.

"Asshole," Shane mumbled under his breath. I rolled my eyes and reached for the bag Shane was carrying. I thanked my lucky stars; he had brought my fleece socks, yoga pants, one of his hooded sweatshirts, and my e-reader. "What did he want?" Shane folded back the blanket and gently pulled the fleece socks over my frosty toes. Gratefully, I reveled in their warmth.

"He wanted to check on me. Oh, and he gave me the gist of the police report." I filled Shane in on the details Tommy had given me. I also included the part about the Cruz Cartel.

Shane rubbed his face tiredly. "It just sounds too good to be true. It's entirely way too convenient."

Too exhausted to argue, I shrugged. "I'm going by what Tommy told me. He hasn't given me any reason to distrust him." Then I quickly changed the subject. "I appreciate the bag. Thanks."

"You're most certainly welcome, although I can't take the credit. Your mom packed it. She mumbled something about how a man can live with only an extra pair of boxers and how guys can't pack to save their lives."

I laughed. "Mom is so right. Before Dad passed away, he would go on his 'boys' weekends.' He would only pack beer and enough underwear to last him until he came home. No socks, no jackets, no pants. And when he came home, Mom would make him undress in the garage because he reeked of booze, smoke, and the woods. Of course, he'd weasel his way in and chase Mom all around the house trying to give her 'the stinky hug'. It was so gross and hilarious at the same time."

"Yeah, well. I know your mom well enough to know that I will never win an argument with her. So I will just nod my head, smile, and do what I'm told."

I smiled. "She's trained you well. That's good."

"She also packed some chicken soup and some of your seltzer water." As he poured the soup into a bowl, his eyes turned to me. "Oh, by the way, I found out about the blue box."

I choked on my water and coughed at the mention of the blue velvet jewelry box, the box that contained my mother's white gold one-carat diamond engagement ring. "Hey, I'm sorry about that. The last thing you need is pressure from her—"

Shane's laugh stopped me in mid-sentence. "Come on, Megs. Do you honestly think I would trek across the country to make sure you're okay and *not* marry you? Of course I want to propose, and thanks to your mom, I have a ring to do it with. But that doesn't mean I'm going to do it right now, or anytime soon for that matter. Let's get home and get this mess we're dealing with straightened out, and then we'll talk about it."

He left me speechless. "Right. Of course," I stuttered, my mind already filled with images of dresses, rings, and white. The confirmation of his intentions eased what was left of my anxiety about our future. *This is the man I am going to marry.*

CHAPTER 7

AFTER A SLEEPLESS NIGHT, I was discharged early the next morning with a prescription for prescription strength Tylenol and strict orders to stay in bed for the next few days. My mom, Aunt Karen, and Uncle Bob waited in the kitchen while Shane made sure I was settled in bed, then he hurriedly got dressed in order to make it to his interview with Tommy on time.

"Are you sure you want me to go?" Shane asked, straightening the navy-blue tie. "I'm sure Tommy can reschedule this. I mean hell, he waited this long; he can wait a little while longer." The gray pinstriped suit looked amazing on him and was cut perfectly across his broad shoulders. He looked like he had just stepped out of *GQ* magazine. I mentally wiped the drool from my lips.

"Better to do it now and get it over with. Besides, I can't ravage you anyway. I'm stuck in bed with orders to remain chaste and can barely move." I smacked the pillow beside me in frustration. "The only thing to do today is watch TV and listen to my aunt and mom cluck over me like chickens. I'm just sorry I can't be with you," I grumbled.

"I know. I hate leaving you like this." He leaned down on the bed. His soft goatee tickled my skin as he nuzzled my neck.

I closed my eyes and slowly leaned my head back, giving him as much as he wanted. My hands clutched his head, holding him there. His groan vibrated against the most sensitive part of my neck, causing my body to grow hot. Knowing that the bed rest order wouldn't last forever, I took pleasure in torturing him. I ran my fingernails through his hair, sending his body into quivers. Shifting his weight, Shane eased himself closer until his lips found mine open for him. Our tongues clashed, our kiss deepening, as his suit-covered erection pressed into my hip. With my blood boiling and the ache ever increasing, I ran my hand down his body to feed his need, cupping what was hidden from my sight.

"My God, Megan, you're going to be the death of me," he muttered, pulling back.

I gave him my most innocent smile. "You started it.

I'm just giving as good as I got."

"You're trouble. That's what you are." He smoothed his hair down again and adjusted his pants. "I need a cold shower. Your uncle is going to take one look at me and think I'm a pervert or something."

"Think hockey. Think of Mrs. Saunders from across the street," I said helpfully, naming our eighty-six-year-old neighbor.

Shane shivered. "That'll do it." He turned at the knock on the door. "And there are your nurses, impatiently waiting for me to leave so they can dote on their patient." He leaned over for quick kiss. "I love you, babe. I'll be home soon." Shane opened the door to my waiting aunt and mom, their arms crossed. "She's all yours," he said with a smile. He winked at me, then gave the ladies a wide berth as he sidled out. I smiled dutifully, mentally counting the minutes until he'd be back. My mom and Aunt Karen were wonderful, but they could be overbearing at times.

After an hour of assuring my nurses that I was fine and that, no, I didn't need pain medication, they finally left me alone. Penny was my lone companion, sleeping on her bed with her woobie tucked beside her. I watched reruns and waddled gingerly to the bathroom, but by the time three o'clock came around, I was bored out of my mind.

I awoke to the sound of Shane's voice downstairs,

then the kitchen door closing. A few minutes later, his large frame appeared in the doorway.

"Hey," I said sleepily, "how did it go?"

"All right, I guess. I answered all their questions and they expunged my record. I'm no longer a convicted felon," he said with a grin. He took off his tie and dropped it on the chair. "How are you feeling?"

"Like I got hit by a car," I smirked. "I'm okay, just sore. Katie is moving around nicely, making sure she gets all her favorite spots." I replied, rubbing the mound on my stomach, presumably her rear end.

"That's good. Do you want some dinner? Your mom made butternut squash soup." My stomach instantly growled. "I'll take that as a yes. As soon as I change I'll bring some up."

Shane shucked off his suit pants and pulled off his navy shirt. The sight of his lean, muscular body sent an immediate shiver down my spine. The man was delicious, pure and simple. I wanted nothing more than to lick him all over, wanted to feel him inside of me, clenched between my legs. The image of him underneath me sent my body into overdrive. But thanks to my physical limitations and Dr. DeVaughn's strict "no sex for one week" order, my need for Shane would have to go unfulfilled. Groaning, I pushed myself up into a sitting position.

"What's wrong? Do you need to get up?" Shane

asked, rushing to my side.

"Yeah, I need to take a shower," I grumbled. I knew a cold shower would be the only relief I would get at the moment. I gave a pointed look at the tent protruding from his boxer briefs and shook my head when he went to remove them. "By myself," I said. "I don't trust that thing anywhere near me right now. I don't think I can say no."

Chuckling, Shane walked over and pulled my nightshirt over my head. "Baby, I'm the king of self-control right now. As much as I would love to have you naked and screaming my name, I also know that you're hurting. Plus, I heard what the doctor said. Trust me; the wait will be worth it." His hand gently cupped my overflowing breasts. Sucking air in between my teeth, I steeled myself against the onslaught of arousal that began to course through my veins. *This is the female version of blue balls, I'm sure of it.*

"Argh! Seriously? You're such a pain!" I rolled my eyes and pushed him back. I walked stiffly into the bathroom and turned the water on as hot as it could go. I knew a cold shower would cure my craving for Shane, but a hot shower would help with the soreness in my back.

I stood in the shower, the water easing the tension from my aching muscles. After drying off and changing into another nightshirt, I slid into bed right as Shane brought in a tray of food. The aroma of cinnamon and nutmeg sent my stomach into a frenzy.

"This smells amazing. Thank you," I said, pulling open the cracker pack he offered me. The piping hot soup was exactly what I needed. "You're not going to eat?"

"I'm good. Your uncle took me to Adam's for a late lunch," Shane replied with a smirk. I scowled at the thought of him enjoying my favorite pulled pork without me.

I finished my soup and set the bowl aside. We settled in to watch the Food Network, which is not a good show to watch while pregnant. Even though I'd already eaten, watching Bobby Flay prepare steak nachos on the screen sent my cravings into overdrive. I wiped the drool from my mouth. Shane looked over at me, laughter in his eyes.

"Mmmm, nachos," I whispered. A resounding thump vibrated my lower belly. I absentmindedly rubbed the spot.

"Do you want nachos?" he asked, raising an eyebrow.

"Nah. I'm good. I don't need it," I replied loftily, trying to convince myself.

"Okay, the better question—does Katie want nachos?" he whispered to the rounded lump. The visible kick from the inside of my stomach was all Shane needed. Smiling, he rose off the bed and said, "You don't have a choice. The baby wants nachos. I'll be right back." He bounded down the stairs in search of chips and salsa.

Sighing, I leaned back against the pillows. This seemed so easy, so…so normal. But a lump of foreboding seemed to have permanently lodged in my throat. The question was, how long would this normal last?

CHAPTER 8

AS THE DAYS WENT BY, everything seemed to work itself out. After a satisfactory visit with Dr. DeVaughn, I was released from bed rest. That, along with Shane's slow venture into society, gave us a sense of normalcy. It was easy for us to fall back into a routine, albeit with caution.

Shane's paranoia of the Cruz Cartel had not died. While his demeanor slowly returned to normal, a look of unease clung to him. He became more guarded than he ever was before, suspiciously eyeing every passerby and SUV. He accepted Tommy's presence in my life with apprehension. Truly, Shane had no choice in the matter. Tommy had saved my life, and I wasn't about to push him away because my boyfriend didn't like him. If anything, Tommy's ability to track the cartel should've given Shane a sense of comfort. But it didn't.

The cartel's silence had led us to a sense of security, but Shane insisted that extra measures needed to be taken. Our alarm system was upgraded, motion lights were added to the exterior, and the doors were fitted with security bars. I knew Shane always carried his Glock, although words were never spoken on the subject and it was doubtful that he had the proper permits.

We picked out a new car. Well, a year-old black Ford Edge, to be exact. Shane wanted me to drive a tank, but an SUV was a good compromise. Shane went back to work at Adrian's auto and bike repair shop, resuming his late night hours. When he wasn't working, he scoured the Internet for any new information on the cartel. Always watching, always waiting for something to happen. We came up with a plausible story for his return in case anyone asked; being in a federal prison made the most sense. Aside from those in our inner circle, no one— whether it was someone from Adrian's shop, gossip hounds, or the neighbors—knew that Shane had been in the safe house. Some people were skeptical about the prison story and asked questions, but for the most part, the general public wasn't concerned with his return.

Days turned into weeks. Shane and I spent Thanksgiving at Mom's house, nestled into a coma induced by roasted turkey, peppery stuffing, and football. It felt good to sit and relax. Between our busy work schedules and my all-consuming exhaustion, we rarely spent any real time together. I begged off the family's annual Black Friday shopping spree and we headed home before the tryptophan turned us into zombies.

Once we got home and settled in for the night, a new burst of energy kicked in. Fully into my third trimester, I now moved slower and had a lot less energy. But my hormones were through the roof and my sexual need was rarely satiated for long. Unfortunately, the big belly made achieving the ultimate goal very awkward. We'd become creative at finding just the right position. In awe of my ever-changing body, Shane hadn't been able to keep his hands off me. I didn't mind one bit because I craved his touch more than any other craving I'd ever had.

I watched Shane as he undressed and climbed into the shower. Desire pooled low in my belly and the need to feel him overwhelmed me. I stripped quickly and opened the glass door to the steam shower where I joined him under the rain of hot water.

Wordlessly, I took the soap from his hands and ran the bar over his chiseled pectoral muscles and down his toned abs. The sharp intake of breath between his teeth brought a smile to my face as I placed the soap on the holder and gripped his rigid shaft with one hand. I pulled his face down to mine with my other hand and slid my tongue inside his mouth, stroking his throbbing cock. Shane wrapped his arms around me, crushing me to his chest. The heat from the steam and the slickness between us had my blood boiling. Shane pulled back slightly, disengaging my hand from his erection. Disappointed, I looked up into his hazel eyes.

"I'm about to burst and when I do, it will be inside you." His voice low with arousal had me dripping with anticipation. I turned off the water and stepped out, grabbing my towel.

"I need you inside me," I said bluntly. The intense ache made my legs clench. I dried off quickly then hurried over to the bed with Shane right on my heels. Grabbing me from behind, his hands quickly went to work, cupping my aching sex in one hand and kneading my breast with the other. His hard need pressed against my behind as I leaned forward on the bed, giving him the opening he needed. Shane's fingers worked slowly, brushing against my clit, moving the tender nub in a circular motion. My breath hitched as I came closer to exploding. I mewed with frustration as his finger left me until he bent me over farther. Holding my hips tightly, he glided his cock inside me. Wet with need, my body expanded to allow his girth to completely fill me. I met every thrust with a push of my own, riding the wave until stars appeared before my eyes. With a scream, I succumbed to the ecstasy and my body went limp with exhaustion.

Shane eased himself off me and helped me up. "Now I can go to sleep," I quipped. Chuckling, he cleaned me up and slipped a tank top over my head. I climbed into bed and watched as he pulled on a pair of sweats and his socks. I frowned with confusion. "Why are you getting dressed?"

"Not tired. Feel like rolling to Adrian's for a bit," he muttered, slipping on his sneakers.

"It's eleven o'clock on Thanksgiving night. Why don't you wait until tomorrow?" Taken aback, the shift in his attitude had me concerned. Why, all of a sudden, was it so important for him to go tonight?

"You're going to sleep right?" Shane asked pointedly. I nodded. "Well, it's either hang out around here and putz around on the computer, or I can go to the shop and get some work done. The shop is behind on repairs and Adrian's offering time and a half for anyone working the holiday weekend."

"Hey, I'm just curious why this is suddenly coming up now. Why didn't you mention anything earlier?"

Shane sighed with exasperation. "I don't know, Megan. Maybe because I figured I would be tired. Or we'd stay at your mom's longer. If this is such an issue, I'll stay. That's fine. We don't need the money or anything."

Are you fucking kidding me? My blood simmered with irritation. I held up my hands and said, "Lose the damn attitude. I was just wondering. I don't care what you do. Just go."

I was too pissed to look at him anymore and rolled onto my side, drawing the duvet up over my ears.

"Megs—" he started but I cut him off.

"Make sure the alarm is on when you leave."

With my eyes closed tight and my breath held, I listened as I heard him shut the door softly. Once I heard the chime of the activated alarm, I allowed the tears prickling behind my eyelids to fall freely. The fact that he left didn't bother me. Hell, I understood. It was the tone of his voice and his attitude that concerned me. It was reminiscent of when Shane had first moved in, when he always went out during the late night hours, when he was dealing for the cartel and working as a narc for the FBI. *Is this just a preview of what's to come?* I pushed the potential angst out of my mind. *No. We'll get through this. We'll talk it through tomorrow.*

***

I woke up early to an empty bed. Not terribly unusual; Shane had a habit of not getting in until after the sun comes came up. But it ticked me off to think that it didn't bother him that I had been upset. Lambasting him as soon as he walked through the door had been my initial plan, but knowing both of our tempers, I knew it wouldn't solve anything.

I shrugged on my bathrobe and padded down the stairs with Penny in tow. I started the coffee and searched the fridge for something to eat. The aroma of the percolating hazelnut brew filled the room. I longed for the sweet, gooey, goodness of my mother's famous cinnamon rolls, but Dr. DeVaughn's words, "gestational diabetes" and "lower carbohydrate diet," echoed in my head. I had just pulled out the eggs and spinach to set about making an omelet, when my phone rang.

Once I looked at the number, my eyes widened in surprise. While hearing from Tommy on a regular basis had become standard, him calling at seven thirty in the morning wasn't.

"Hey, Tommy," I answered as I whisked the egg and spinach mixture.

"Megan, I'm sorry to be calling you so early."

"What's going on?" My gut clenched with worry. Was it Shane? Had something happened to him?

"Shane was locked up this morning."

CHAPTER 9

I DROPPED THE WHISK into the bowl, splattering raw eggs and spinach onto the counter. "What the hell happened? Is he okay?"

"Yeah. It was a street fight that got him arrested, but that's not the worst of it. He was caught with an ounce of marijuana, which is a misdemeanor with a thousand dollar fine. With his record now clean and your uncle representing him, he shouldn't get any time."

I inhaled a shaky breath and sat down at the table. "What the hell happened? Where was he? Where is he now? Do I have to go and get him?"

"According to the Baltimore PD, he was arrested in Fells Point outside the clubs on Broadway. Shane was arrested along with two other guys, a Miguel Santori and a Donald Marcos. As soon as the PD pulled them apart, they clammed up. No reason was given for their brawl. All three of them went before Judge McMahon this morning. Luckily for Shane, the judge had a full docket and set bail relatively low. I'm picking him up now at central booking," Tommy explained.

Knowing Shane was okay and not dead in an alley somewhere allowed whatever relief I felt to turn into fury. The bastard lied to me. He specifically told me that he was going to the shop. And last I checked, the shop wasn't in Baltimore's Fells Point. *Why the hell was he carrying pot? Is he dealing again? Who the hell are these guys that he was with?* Lost in my own thoughts and anger, I forgot that Tommy was still on the line.

"Tommy, I'll bring him home."

"Megs, I know you're mad. But think about it. It won't do you any good to storm up there and demand answers. You're too keyed up right now. I'm sure he's climbing the walls, ready to get out. Let me bring him home."

"He hates your guts, Tommy. Why would you do that?" I said bluntly.

"Because I would rather risk his wrath than have you go there, rip him to shreds, and say things you'll probably regret. If I bring him home it will give you both time to cool down." Tommy answered calmly. He was right, of course. Cool heads should prevail and I was heated with rage. Breathing out a long sigh, I agreed and told Tommy I'd see him soon. I hung up the phone and gripped my cup of coffee. My appetite was gone, and I fought hard to remain calm. The questions and "what if" scenarios ran through my head like a movie.

After stewing in my own thoughts for a few minutes, I headed upstairs to change, knowing that I'd be more comfortable in an argument if I was wearing clothes instead of pajamas., I waddled back downstairs just as the kitchen door was being unlocked. Momentarily forgetting my anger, I rushed over to the door as Shane walked in. I gasped when I took in the bruises on his face. His right eye was swollen and already turning purple. The cut on his lip stood out against the five-day growth of his goatee. But that wasn't the worst. The worst was the dark stare he gave me as he tried to brush past me.

"Wait a minute. We need to talk about this," I said sharply, grabbing his arm.

He pulled back quickly. "I'm beat. I'm going to bed. We'll talk later." Shane snapped, then stalked across the room and up the stairs without a word. Speechless, I looked at Tommy with my mouth gaping.

"Let him sleep it off, Megs. He'll be okay." Tommy reassured me.

Yeah, but will we be okay?

"I have to run. I'll call you later." He gave me a quick

peck on the forehead and closed the door behind him.

Frustrated at the lack of answers, I quickly called my Uncle Bob.

"Hi, Uncle Bob."

"Hey, Megs. I was just about to call you. Have you spoken with Shane?" he asked.

Getting straight to the point I see. "Actually, I was going to ask you the same question. Apparently there was an incident this morning," I said cautiously.

"I'm aware. I spoke with Shane this morning and I wired the money for the bail. However, he didn't want me to pick him up. Were you able to get him home?"

"No. Tommy gave him a ride home. I didn't hear anything about it until Tommy called me this morning," I replied, my voice cracking with frustration.

"Hmmm. In any case, we have a hearing in December to discuss the charges. He will probably be put on probation and will have to pay a fine, but I don't believe we're looking at jail time."

"Thanks, Uncle Bob, for everything. How much was his bail? I can pay you back," I stated, wondering how on earth I could ever repay him for his care and generosity.

He coughed awkwardly and said. "Don't worry about it. Consider this part of my pro bono work."

Gratefully, I repeated my thanks and promised to have Shane call him back once he woke up. With my head full of questions and the answers sleeping upstairs, I walked around the living room, anxious for something to do. I combed the Internet for baby gear and Christmas presents until my hand cramped, then I threw the ball for Penny and flipped through the TV channels until exhaustion overtook me.

After a two-hour nap on the couch, I awoke to find Penny staring up the stairs. "What's up, Pen?" I said groggily, brushing a strand of hair out of my face. The sound of footsteps upstairs caused me to bolt up into a sitting position just as Shane began coming down the stairs.

"Hi," I said pointedly.

His closely cut brown hair glistened from the shower and his hazel eyes widened in surprise. "Oh, hey. I didn't think you were home."

"Where else would I be?" I asked, incredulous.

Shane shrugged and walked into the kitchen, opening the refrigerator door. "I don't know. The mall, I guess. Your mom's."

"Are you serious? You get arrested and don't tell me anything about it, and you think the perfect place for me is the mall? Come on, Shane. Give me a little bit of credit."

Slamming the fridge door shut, he turned around with a defiant look on his face.

"Let it go, Megan," he shot back.

"Let it go? Are you fucking kidding me? I was worried sick about your sorry ass. I deserve some answers. What the hell happened? Why were you in Baltimore? Why were you in a fight? What is up with the weed? And why the hell did you lie to me?" I demanded, the questions falling like water.

"Why bother?" he snapped, slumping on the kitchen table.

"Why bother? Because I'm worried, Shane! You've worked so damn hard to get your record clean, so why fuck it up now? I don't understand what's going with you. Terrible things are going through my head right now, Shane. Don't make me think the worst." Tears of frustration welled up in my eyes.

"Thanks, Megan, for your vote of confidence," he snapped defensively.

"Goddamnit, Shane, I'm tired of walking on fucking egg shells around you. You're moody as hell, you're lying to me, heck – I don't even have your attention most of the time. I have no clue what to think, and that scares the ever-living hell out of me. You need to talk to me." I grabbed his face and forced him to look into my eyes. All I saw was sadness and disgrace. "I love you. I believe in you. But you have to tell me the truth. No more lies."

"I'm doing the only thing I know to do, and that's protecting what's mine!" he roared. He turned away, shoving the kitchen chair violently.

"Then talk to me! Tell me what's going on. I can't be on your side if I'm left in the dark." I said softly. His shoulders sagged in defeat, as if the will to fight had been drained from his warrior body. I tugged him into the family room and sat on the couch, pulling him down with me. "What's going on?"

Shane rubbed his face vigorously, as if he were trying to wake up. "I haven't been working overtime at Adrian's shop. I've been out looking for any information I can find on the cartel."

"Okay. Why?"

"Because they're still out there. They tried to kill you and the baby. They almost killed me. Do you honestly think I can let them get away with that? I know they are still out there. They are hiding, just waiting for the right time to strike. Those guys that I was fighting? Drug pushers. I was trying to get some information on the cartel."

My heart pounded. "You need to just leave it alone, Shane. If you know something, tell Tommy. Let the FBI handle this. Don't do this on your own."

"I can't trust them Megan! There is a fucking leak inside that organization, there has to be. It was because of them the safe house was torched and those men died. It was because of them you were in that gunfight at Deep Creek Lake. All the information concerning our whereabouts was supposed to be a secret, not known to anyone outside Tommy's group, and yet we were fucking targeted. The cartel knew exactly where we were. "

"Shane, this is dangerous. We just got you back. We can't lose you again. I'm begging you. Please leave the cartel alone. Who's to say that once they find out where you are, they won't come around looking for you, looking for us? We're not on their radar. Why are you bringing the fight home?"

"They don't know I'm back," was Shane's steely reply.

"Oh, yeah. What happens when those guys you fought with go running back to the cartel, huh? Hell, for all we know, the cartel is on its way here now. Do they know you're the narc?" Panicked, I looked toward the kitchen door, waiting for the knob to turn.

"No. They don't know me, and they didn't hear me give my name to the cops. Miguel and Don are small-time pushers that don't matter too much. I wanted to see if the cartel has ventured into something else besides coke and heroin. These guys were trying to sell me a crap product with a designer price tag. When I balked, that's when the fight broke out."

"Tommy says that the cartel is a mess. Reggie is dead. How can you be sure the cartel is up and running?" I demanded.

"The cartel isn't as disorganized as Tommy thinks. I've been hearing things that prove otherwise. Plus, Kate—"

"Kate? You've been talking to Kate?" I interrupted. I was surprised that he'd been talking to her. Kate was Tommy's old partner and Shane's former handler who had pretended to be his girlfriend in the beginning of this whole mess.

"Well, yeah. You left your computer open and I was up late one night. Your Skype chirped and, well, we just started talking. She's been working the cartel angle down in Miami."

"She never mentioned it to me. We used to talk pretty frequently but it's been a while."

"When I talked to her last week she said that she was coming up for the holidays," he replied nonchalantly.

He talked to her last week? Why am I only hearing about this now? What else is he keeping from me?

"Did you tell Tommy any of this?" I asked, already tired from this inquisition.

"No. I'd rather Kate tell him. She was his partner. If I say anything I'll look like the paranoid asshole."

"So why were you lying to me? Why not tell me the truth? I would have understood."

"Because you wouldn't have let me go out there and I wasn't sure what I would find. I didn't want to tell you and then be totally wrong." Shane said, rubbing my hand absentmindedly.

I squeezed his hand. "Shane, I would have stopped you because I am scared. Because we need to let it go and let the FBI handle it. Did you find what you were looking for?"

"I think so. I need to go over it with Kate, but I think we have enough for the FBI to pay attention."

"How did you get so much information? What else have you been doing?" I questioned.

Shane sighed. "Listening. It's amazing what people say when they're stoned or drunk. People get sloppy."

Another wave of fear came over me. "Shane, what do you want to happen with this information? What is this going to do to us? Are they going to come after you again? Are we going to be safe?"

Shane gripped my hand and stared into my eyes. "No. This will not blow back on us. Talking with Don and Miguel last night—that was it. I got antsy, bored. I swear, that's the only time. The rest has just been me following a few people, staking out common spots, listening to them talk amongst themselves. No one has seen me; we're safe." Worry consumed my heart as I struggled to trust in Shane's assurances.

How can he be so sure?

CHAPTER 10

THE NEXT COUPLE DAYS were rough. While I wanted to talk to Tommy about the cartel situation, I respected Shane's request to stay quiet. It was easy to understand why he wanted to keep it close, but at the same time I believed that if Tommy knew, he could allay Shane's fears.

Every time Shane left the house alone I would wonder if today would be the day the cartel would find him again. It infuriated me that we were once again looking over our shoulders. Our relationship became strained, to say the least. The thick tension in the house squelched any more spontaneous lovemaking, and as the pregnancy dragged on, I lost the desire.

But I knew we couldn't go on like this forever.

Christmas was coming and usually the holidays put me in a festive spirit, but this year had gotten off to a gloomy start. I didn't want to start the season like a Grumpy Gus so I decided to spice things up a bit. I thought that a nice dinner, some candlelight, and maybe some fireworks would heat up our cold spell. So I left work early and headed to Wegmans. Once I had all the ingredients I needed for chicken potpie and apple turnovers, I steered my shopping cart toward the checkout.

"Hello, Megan."

The southern baritone voice stopped me in my tracks. I slowly turned around and, lo and behold, there he was—Alex Collins. A year ago, when I was lonely and pretending that I wasn't interested in Shane, I met Alex at a Starbucks. He was charming, had beautiful gray eyes, and a brilliant smile. We hit it off pretty well, until I learned that his charm was as fake as my favorite Chanel bag. Beneath that caramel-colored skin and those tight abs was a lying, cheating, douche bag. We had a good thing going for about a month, until I found that Alex had a wife, a fact he neglected to tell me about before he stuck his tongue down my throat. *Bitter? No, I'm not bitter. But I do hold a grudge.*

I raised an eyebrow and looked over his warm-up pants and hooded sweatshirt with disdain. I hadn't seen him in almost a year and, boy, time sure does change one's perception. He didn't look as gorgeous as I remembered, probably because I was no longer impressed with his charm or sexy voice. Or maybe it was because he played me for a fool.

"Hello, Alex," I replied coolly and turned my attention to the items on the conveyor belt ahead of me.

"You're looking...uh...well," he faltered as he gestured to my increased girth.

"I am doing absolutely amazing. Thank you."

"That's good to hear."

He paused awkwardly, unsure of what to say next. I mentally implored the woman in front of me to hurry up, but, of course, the supervisor had to be called over for a twenty-cent price difference.

"So, you're expecting, huh? That's great."

I groaned under my breath. *Really? Do we have to do this? It's bad enough that I have to stand next to him in line, but do we really need to make small talk?* I nodded as I fought the urge to give the cashier a quarter just to hurry things along.

"That's right. I'm due in February."

"Wow. You must be having twins!" he blurted out. His eyes widened as soon as the words left his mouth.

Are you fucking kidding me? Apparently his mental filter wasn't working. I glared at him. "Excuse me?"

"I'm sorry. I didn't mean...You look beautiful, of course, just totally different from the last time I saw you. It wasn't that long ago, so I just assumed..." The normally suave-and-collected Alex became flustered, and with good reason; I'm sure I resembled a cartoon character with steam coming out of its ears.

"Really. You haven't seen me in months and the first thing you ask me is if I'm having twins? Would you say that to any other pregnant woman? Would you say that to your *wife?*" I demanded. The gall of the bastard to say anything to me at all, let alone something as moronic as this, made me want to pick up the chicken in my cart and throw it at him.

"Uh…I…no, I guess not." The boy looked scared, almost enough to wet himself. Alex backed away slightly, bumping into a passerby's cart.

"If you wouldn't say it to your *wife,* Alex, you sure as hell shouldn't say it to anyone else. Speaking of your wife, have you told her how you're a sad, pathetic excuse for a husband yet?" I asked, my words dripping with venom. Screw being lady-like. I wanted to kick his behind all the way to the deli counter.

"I'm sorry, truly I am. I didn't mean anything by it. B-b-but hey, I forgot the bread. It was nice seeing you again, Megan." And with that, he turned tail and scurried away.

"Asshole," I muttered as I watched him disappear.

"You don't look like you're having twins," the young cashier remarked as she rang up my groceries. I smiled in thanks, but my good mood had deflated. *Stupid Alex.*

Once home, I put the groceries away and put the chicken in the oven. I sent a quick text message to Shane telling him about dinner and headed upstairs to change out of my too-tight maternity clothes. My usual attire of yoga pants and a T-shirt wasn't ideal for the romance I had planned, but my wardrobe choices were diminishing. I exhaled as I searched for something that could be sexy. Finally, I grabbed one of Shane's oversized white dress shirts and a matching bra and boyshort set. My stomach fluttered with nervous energy, as if this were going to be our first time. I straightened up the bedroom, throwing everything into the closet. After selecting the right playlist for the evening, I went downstairs into the kitchen for some matches and lit several small votive candles, setting them around the room. I was going for some ambience, but knowing my bad luck, I'd trip over something, so I didn't leave the room too dark.

I had just started peeling the sweet potatoes when Shane's ringtone filled the air. Anticipation overcame my body and I eagerly picked up the phone.

"Hey, baby, I was just thinking about you," I said in what I hoped was my let's-get-it-on-right-now voice.

"Oh, yeah? I've been thinking about you all day. But I have some bad news. We're completely swamped. I'm going to be late for dinner."

Disappointment coursed over me like a cold wave.

"Oh." *Well, hell, why did I shave my legs then?*

"I'm sorry, Megs, but Adrian needs me."

I couldn't contain my bitterness. "And I don't? Let me ask you this, Shane: does Adrian really need you, or is this another way of saying you're going out cartel hunting?" Silence answered my question and disappointment filled my voice. "I should have expected this. I haven't seen you in what feels like forever. We barely talk anymore. You're either at the damn shop or you're out hunting down the cartel. But whatever. Do what you need to do. I'll be here, as always, waiting for you."

"Don't act like that, Megs," Shane pleaded.

"Don't act like what? Someone who misses her boyfriend? Take a step back and look at this from my perspective. I'm pregnant. I'm lonely. And I have a damn chicken in the oven. If you're not home in an hour, then I'm eating without you."

Shane was quiet. "Baby, I'm sorry. I know I haven't been around much. I'm trying, though. I really am."

Sadness crept in. "You say you are, and damn, Shane, I want to believe you. You said you trekked across the country to be with me, but yet here I am, waiting. If I'm not a priority now, when will I be?"

"Megan, that's not right and you know it," he shot back.

"Says the man that is not home with his pregnant

girlfriend. I understand the need for revenge Shane, I really do. But not at the cost of those who are important, namely you and Katie," I replied, disappointment evident in my voice.

I ended the call and wiped away the tears of frustration as the candlelight flickered. *Well, no need for these anymore.* I blew out the candles and headed upstairs to change back into my normal attire. The desire to make the night special had been squashed.

After washing the mascara streaks from my face, I went downstairs to finish making dinner. Whether Shane would be home to eat it or not was up to him. Once I had put the potatoes on the burner and set the timer, all Penny and I could do was wait.

I reflected on our conversation and grimaced. I hated fighting with Shane and now that I was calm enough, I could see why he was struggling with how to move forward. Being back in the thick of a difficult situation would be tough on anyone. He was being torn; one side of him wanted to go vigilante to protect our family, and the other wanted to forget the past and move on. He's never been the type of person to brush things off, to let things go. But in order for us to move on from this, to be the family that we're supposed to be, something's going to have to give. And I'm sure as hell not giving up on him. On us.

CHAPTER 11

M Y HEAD SNAPPED UP and I wiped the drool from my chin. *When did I fall asleep?* My eyes widened as the fog lifted and I heard the microwave timer go off. *Oh no! The potatoes!* I hurried into the kitchen and turned off the burner. Thankfully, the potatoes weren't too overdone. Glancing at the timer on the oven, I was relieved to see that the roast chicken still had ten minutes. *Holy shit. I almost burned dinner!*

My thoughts were interrupted by a knock at the door.

What now? I shook the cobwebs out of my head as I shuffled over to the door. I pulled back the curtain that covered the window on the door and let out a gasp. Standing under my carport with a bag full of Christmas gifts was none other than Kate Parker.

"Oh my goodness! Come in, come in!" I cried, throwing open the door. Gorgeous as always with her petite frame and stunning ice-blue eyes, Kate looked exactly as I remembered her. Well, except that her light-brown hair was now a striking chestnut brown with maroon highlights.

"Good gracious, woman, you're huge!" I rolled my eyes and I pulled her into a hug. Kate is one of the few people, aside from Jen and Sarah, who can get away with commenting on my girth, especially after Alex's stupid comment.

"You're lucky I love you. When did you get to town? Shane told me you were coming, but he didn't say when."

Kate draped her black leather jacket over the kitchen chair and sat down. "A few days ago. I had to finish up a few things in Miami and I didn't know when I would be done."

"How long are you staying around?" I asked as I started the coffeemaker. Kate had a never-ending craving for caffeine and could drink it day or night. I came around to the table and sat down next to her. Dressed in a fitted, blue V-neck sweater and dark-rinse jeans, she looked just as intimidating as she did when I first met her. Collected, stylish, and beautiful—she was everything I wasn't. I used to be jealous of Kate, but we'd gone through so much together—including Kate putting herself in harm's way to save me—that my jealousy gave way to a genuine affection for her. She'd become one of my best friends. It's amazing what a little rain of gunfire can do for a friendship.

Kate shrugged. "Not sure. At least for the next couple of weeks. I have a few meetings at FBI Headquarters next week, then Cole and I are headed to the folk's house for Christmas."

Interest piqued, I leaned forward to get the gossip. "Cole, huh? You didn't tell me you met someone."

Confusion crossed over Kate's face and then she burst into laughter.

"Cole? No way! He's my brother."

Now it was my turn to be perplexed. "I thought you had a sister."

Shaking her head, she replied, "Oh I do. I have a sister. Well, I guess she's my stepsister. Charlie is twenty-three and she lives with my mom and stepdad. My stepbrother, Cole, got out of the Navy last summer and lives around here. I'm staying with him until we go to Essex to see our parents."

Kate got up and helped herself to a mug from the cabinet, poured a cup of coffee, and came back to the table with a questioning look on her face.

"Where's Shane?"

The oven timer went off, giving me time to think

of an answer. *How much did she know? What had Shane told her?* I debated what to say while I pulled the bird out of the oven. I didn't want to give too much away or give her false information. After turning off the oven and leaving the door open to let the heat warm up the kitchen, I leaned against the counter, apprehensive.

Kate read me like a book and cocked her head. "What happened?"

"How often have you talked with Shane?" I countered.

"About once a week or so. Why? What's up?" Something clicked and she nodded knowingly. "It's about the cartel isn't it?"

"Yes! And I don't understand! I mean, okay, I do get it. He wants revenge and, shit, he deserves redemption, and I understand that! But why can't he just tell Tommy? Why does he have to go traipsing around Fells Point?" I demanded in exasperation. I filled my glass with water and sat down at the table with a harrumph.

Kate's eyes filled with pity as she squeezed my hand. "I know, hon. It sucks. And trust me, I've tried to convince Shane to let me and Rick handle the cartel, but the boy is hell-bent on doing it himself."

I paused. Rick was the third member of Tommy's group. "You said you and Rick. What about Tommy?" I asked.

I could see the wheels turning in Kate's head.

"Tommy is convinced that the cartel is on the outs, despite the small bits of info Rick and I have brought to the table. We're not sure why. Maybe to save face because of the screw up over the summer. The death of those agents was a huge deal, then add Shane coming back from the dead and Tommy looks even more inept. And to be perfectly honest, we never figured out who leaked our location at Deep Creek Lake—and we know it was a leak. Not too many people knew our location. In all honesty, we're trying to keep as much as we can to ourselves, and until we have enough hard evidence to prove that the cartel is back, Tommy will have to listen to us."

"Kate, I'm already paranoid that they're going to grab Shane off the streets. How close is it to reality? How worried should I be?" I asked, panic rising in my voice.

"At this point, you're okay."

"Okay how? I need more than 'okay', Kate. I need someone to tell me that I can stop worrying. Do you know how terrifying it is for me to have to keep looking over my shoulder, to not know if going to the store will be the last thing I do for the rest of my life? I'm having a baby in all this chaos. I don't want to bring her into this world while I'm scared to death that she won't have her parents to raise her!" I cried as I pounded my fist on the table.

Kate jumped, as did her namesake. Kate grabbed

my hand and held it firmly. "Look at me Megan. Baby Katie will be safe. You and Shane are safe. I promise you that."

"How are we safe Kate? I need fucking answers."

Kate sighed. "I've had Cole and his crew running surveillance. It's not on the books and, in fact, it's not with the bureau. It's through some friends that are in the neighborhood. They are keeping their distance, just making sure you're safe."

"What are you not telling me?"

"I've told you everything I know. I'm serious. But the Bureau dropped its surveillance on you and I didn't want to leave you without protection. Cole came back to the area around that time, so I asked him and his friends to look out for you."

"What is this? A hobby for them? Watch after helpless strangers?" I scoffed.

"No, it's their job. Cole's in security and runs a small shop, along with a few other ventures. A lot of what they do is surveillance, monitoring, security detail, and training. It's a little bit of time and they do it when they can, and it pays the bills. Plus, it gives Cole and his buddies a chance to do what they love—beat people up and play with guns," she said with a smile.

I gasped, covering my mouth with my hand and shook my head. "I don't know what to say."

Kate squeezed my hand. "You don't have to say a

thing. I think of you as family, and I protect my family."

The oh-so-familiar sensation prickled behind my eyes again and I hurriedly brushed away the tears. *Damn hormones.*

"Seriously, Kate. We need to work on your people skills. You really need to stop making people cry." Shane's voice came from the doorway of the mudroom. I smiled as I rolled my eyes at the sight of his grease-stained sweatshirt and jeans, and the irresistible grin on his face.

"I only like making you cry, Shane," Kate shot back. She went in for a hug but suddenly pulled back. "Yeah, no thanks. This is a new sweater. I'll save my hug for later."

Shane snickered. "No love. That's fine. I see how you are. I'll go shower and be right down." He brushed passed Kate, who flattened herself against the counter to avoid contact with the grime, and came over to my side. He bent down and gently grazed my ear with his lips. "I'm sorry about dinner. Is everything all right?" His voice was low and tickled one of my most sensitive spots.

My body instantly reacted, growing warm at the touch of his lips despite my mind's protest. *One touch, one freaking whisper of a touch, and I'm putty in his hands. No! Stay mad, Megan. Stay mad!* But I couldn't. I could never stay mad at him. I knew that deep in his heart he meant well. Shane didn't want me to hurt. He was trying his hardest to protect us. I looked into his hazel eyes and nodded.

"It will be," I whispered back to him. *Everything will be okay.*

CHAPTER 12

KATE STAYED FOR DINNER and we chatted late into the evening. We exchanged gifts and she loved the new cashmere scarf we bought her. She also didn't fail to spoil her namesake with a monogrammed quilt. Kate left close to eleven. Afterwards I dozed off on the couch, which was fine with me, as any sort of intimacy had been ruined anyway.

Thankfully, it finally registered with Shane how much time he was spending away from the house. The cartel tracking slowed down. Shane was coming home more often for dinner and a couple times actually stayed with me for an entire weekend. Shocking, to say the least. The entire time he was home I fully expected him to roll out in pursuit of the cartel at any moment.

But he hung in there, through the Christmas shopping and decorating, even through a Rankin-Bass holiday marathon.

But, still, there were mornings where I'd find myself alone in bed, or I'd wake up in the middle of the night to find him gone. Thankfully, it wasn't as frequent, but it still worried me and, frankly, it pissed me off. I didn't like the fact that he kept things from me, that he kept this part of his life hidden. At the same time, though, I knew he needed space, because I would try to talk him out of leaving. I would worry. It was just that, damn, I missed him. I craved those moments together. Not for sex because that was the furthest thing from my mind, but because we only had a limited amount of time before we would have a new member of the family. The time we did spend together felt rushed and tense; not how I had imagined our relationship would be.

We survived Christmas with my family. The bulk of our gifts were addressed to a family member that had not yet arrived. I assured my mom that Katie would love the beautifully stitched stocking and Shane was ecstatic over the new bike jacket I gave him. I received a beautiful charm locket from him, but no ring. My hope for a proposal diminished as the holidays went on.

We spent New Year's Eve with friends and I experienced the sober reality of being a designated driver. It's not so much fun driving slowly down Route

424 with your boyfriend's head hanging out the window. As the last big holiday of non-parenthood came to an end, I was happy to get home and put my feet up while Shane prayed to the porcelain gods.

Soon enough, we took down the tree and put away the decorations. Two weeks into the New Year and a month before my due date, Jen threw us a coed baby shower. At that point, I was done being pregnant. My back ached when I walked, my feet resembled Fred Flintstone's, and my crotch felt like it was ripping in half.

Despite all my pregnancy pains, we went to the party and had a great time. While the women oohed and aahed over the tiny sleepers and discussed breastfeeding equipment, the men huddled around the flat screen TV in Jen's basement, watching the Ravens take on the Redskins.

On our way home, I glanced over at Shane, who was behind the wheel of my SUV. His body was loose and there was a small grin on his face. It was a far cry from the white knuckles on the steering wheel and anxious eyes that I had become used to. Catching my stare, he gave me an impish grin. "What? Do I have food on my face?"

I smiled and placed my hand on his thigh. "You look relaxed. It's nice to see."

"Oh, I'm relaxed. But if you move that hand up,

I'll be even more relaxed," he joked, moving my hand closer to his crotch.

Thanks to the lovely trials of the third trimester, I hadn't felt particularly amorous; it hurt to walk, let alone have intercourse. The very thought of sex had me hiding under the covers. But in that moment heat pooled in my belly as I stroked his erection through the denim fabric while I watched the arousal in his face. Thankfully, there weren't too many cars on Davidsonville Road because the SUV accelerated quickly. Of course, we caught every single red light once we turned onto Route 301.

I continued to stroke against the strain of his zipper. His breath quickened and I relished the power I had in my hand. "Dammit, Meg. You need to stop. I'm going to finish right here," he muttered, groaning as we came to a stop a block from the house.

With a grin that rivaled a cat's that had just eaten a canary, I slowly unzipped his jeans and freed the beast struggling to break out of its denim prison. Shane gasped slightly as I wrapped my fingers around his silky skin. The SUV's engine roared at the green light and the thrust pushed me back into the seat. My core ached, and at that moment I regretted the decision to wear jeans. I needed him to touch me. I needed the release. We arrived at the house, the tires squealing in protest as we lurched to a stop in the driveway. Shane jumped out of the car, his shirt covering his naked appendage, and rushed around to my side, throwing the door open before I could even blink.

Shane didn't hesitate. He helped me down and the second my feet landed on the ground, he pushed me against the car, his lips over mine. His tongue, minty and cool from his gum, prodded and explored my mouth as he pressed his body against mine. I strained to get closer to him but grew frustrated at the space between us. I pulled away from him, breathless, and managed to get out, "Upstairs. Now."

Once inside, he practically ran upstairs. Shane had me by the hand, and I waddled as fast as I could. Shane closed the door and urgently pulled off his clothes, removed mine, and then helped me kneel on the bed. He kissed a trail down my spine, his hot breath feeling like heaven on my skin. I felt him reach for something, but my eyes were closed in ecstasy as I thrilled at his touch. They flew open once I heard the familiar buzzing and I shrieked as I felt a low vibration on my clit. Gasping at the sensation, I turned my head as Shane's tongue gently caressed the tender spot below my ear. He bent me over while maintaining the pressure on my increasingly sensitive nub, sending me soaring just as his swollen cock pushed inside me.

With each thrust and pull, my senses flew into overdrive. Each nerve fired at his touch, sending my body over the cliff. Shane's pelvis pounded into me and our simultaneous screams of ecstasy pierced the night.

Breathing heavily, he pulled out, ignoring my cry of protest, and gingerly helped me turn over onto my back. Still standing, he wrapped my legs around his waist, teasing my entrance with his slick cock.

"Baby, please." I tightened my legs to pull him closer.

Shane's hazel eyes smoldered as he ran his hands down my sides, cupping my behind to lift me up. He grabbed a small pillow and slid it underneath me.

"Don't worry, babe. I got you."

With a grunt, he plunged into me and immediately sent my body into a pleasure spiral, thanks to the new angle. I screamed out his name as I shattered around him. His pace quickened and he climaxed again with a guttural growl.

With our chests heaving and our bodies slick with sweat, Shane rained my face with kisses, then lay down next to me.

"Wow. I missed this," he murmured.

"So did I." I ran my fingers over the ink on his arms as I felt his heart rate slow to normal.

"I love you so much, babe," he whispered and pressed his lips to mine.

"I love you too, but I need to pee. Help me up." Feeling like a beached whale, I struggled to get off the bed on my own. He helped me off the bed, then smacked my ass as I walked away.

As I washed my hands, I stared at my reflection in the mirror. My eyes were bright and my cheeks were flushed with that after-sex glow. I smiled and walked towards the bedroom. I heard another buzzing sounded, although I knew it wasn't of the pleasure variety.

"Yeah?" he said. The conversation drifted into the hallway as I stood just outside the bedroom. "What time?...Fuck. Right now?...Okay, thanks. Give me five minutes." I heard the rustling of his jeans as he pulled them on and then the closet door opening.

My euphoria quickly dissolved to annoyance. *I knew this was too good to last.* I turned and walked back into the bathroom. *Fuck this. I'm going to take a shower and go to bed.* I turned on the water and waited. Waited for Shane to come and apologize for leaving me yet again. Waited for the excuses that I'd heard a hundred times before. Waited for the promise that he would come home soon when we both knew he would break it, that he wouldn't return until the wee hours of the morning. The hot water pulsated against the pain in my lower back. I knew that once he got ahold of something, whether it was a project at the shop or the need to seek out the truth, he wouldn't let it go. It's not in his nature. As the door creaked, I closed my eyes and concentrated on shampooing my hair.

"Hey, babe—"

"I know. You have to go," I said, vigorously scrubbing

shampoo into my long locks. I didn't want to watch him leave. I wasn't sure why, but this departure seemed different from the rest. Unease lay heavy in my stomach. I blindly reached for the conditioner.

"I do. They want my help."

"And you have to go now."

"Yeah."

I ignored the regret in his tone and rinsed my hair. I stepped out and turned to him. Dressed in his usual attire of jeans, a thermal shirt, and a hooded sweatshirt, Shane silently handed me a towel for my hair and then gently dried off my body. I squeezed my eyes shut at the loving gesture. *I know he loves me. I know he's trying to do right by us,* I mentally repeated. But each time he left, I felt like he might never return, and all I would have left of him would be his broken promises.

"If I asked you to stay here and rub my back, would you do it?" I joked wearily, standing naked in front of him. Without saying a word, he gently lifted my chin and brushed my lips with his.

"Of course I would," he whispered.

"Just making sure," I replied nonchalantly. I wanted to beg him, to plead with him to stay, but I knew that if he did stay he would be anxious, like a caged beast on display. He needed to be in on the action and he needed to be there when the truth was uncovered. Shane's tenacity was one of his best qualities — and also one of his worst.

"Be safe out there."

"Always am, babe." He pressed his lips against my forehead and lightly smacked my behind, then walked out of the door. Penny's dog tags jingled as she followed him down the stairs. His truck's engine roared to life and eventually faded away. I shivered, realizing I was still naked in the bathroom. I dressed quickly in yoga pants and Shane's dark-gray hooded sweatshirt and padded downstairs. A sudden craving overcame me, so I preheated the oven for some frozen chocolate turnovers that I had hidden in the freezer. Keeping to the low-carb diet my doctor recommended was hard, and even though I had been good about it, something sweet and chocolaty was exactly what I needed to take my mind off Shane.

Just before the pastries were done, someone knocked at the door. I cautiously looked through the window and recognized Tommy's Suburban. I hadn't seen him in over a month.

"Well, hello there, stranger," I said with a smile, throwing open the door. His green eyes widened as he took in my ever-expanding belly.

"Hello to you too, mama. You look beautiful. About to pop, but beautiful," Tommy replied, kissing my cheek as he entered the house. "Sorry I couldn't make it to the party today, but I got held up at work."

"I totally understand. Thank you for the gift by the way. The wooden boat is really cute."

I led him into the kitchen where the oven timer was going off. After pulling the turnovers out of the oven, I turned off the oven and put the teakettle on the stove.

"I'm glad you liked it. Jessica helped me pick it out," he said casually.

"I want to hear more about this Jessica. You've been spending an awful lot of time with her," I teased, sitting down at the table.

We chatted about his new relationship with Jessica, his caseload, and our lives in general all while I tried desperately not to yawn. We didn't touch on the cartel, which was probably a good thing since there was a risk of my big mouth saying something about Shane.

The teakettle whistled and Tommy quickly got up to make tea and grab plates for our dessert. I gratefully accepted mine, knowing full well how much energy it would have taken for me to get out of the damn chair. *Four more weeks, just four more weeks.* As much as I loved being pregnant, the last month of gas, heartburn, and my pelvis feeling like it's going to crack open wasn't what I pictured pregnancy would be.

"So how are things going with you?" he asked, sipping his tea.

"Things are good. We just have four more weeks left and then this bean will be with us. My last day of work is in about three weeks, so we have a few days to finish everything." I couldn't hold back the yawn any more.

"Where's Shane?"

"At the shop." I didn't want to say anything further, but of course, being the ace FBI agent, he probed just a little bit more.

"He's been working a lot hasn't he? Every time I talk to you, he's at the shop."

I sighed. Tommy was right. During our random phone conversations, Shane was never home.

"He wants to get as much work in as he can so he can spend a week or so with us after Katie's born." I heard the defensiveness in my voice as I spoke. Tommy looked at me with pity in his eyes.

He held his hands up in surrender. "Hey, not judging. Just stating a simple fact that's all."

I rubbed my belly again. The tightness was back and so was the really bad heartburn. "Yeah, I know. Sorry. It's the preggo mood swings. Don't take offense." I yawned again. "I hate to kick you out, Tommy, but I am kicking you out. I need some sleep."

"That's cool. I have to go anyway. I'll talk to you soon, okay?" I followed him to the mudroom door. "Get some rest. Apparently you won't get any after the kid is born." Chuckling, he kissed my cheek and I closed the door behind him.

I locked the door and whistled for Penny to follow

me up the stairs. The day's events had finally worn me down. My stomach hurt, my back ached, and my feet still resembled Fred Flintstone's. I was so exhausted that I took off my pants and didn't bother to put on a nightshirt. I set the alarm and lay on the bed, falling asleep before my head hit the pillow.

CHAPTER 13

Every woman has her ideal birthing scenario, preferably one that's serene and pain free. But then real life happens. And the war stories—all moms have one. And they aren't afraid to tell you and everyone else the graphic details about how long they were in labor and where they were when their water broke.

Despite how exhausted I was and how quickly I had fallen asleep, I opened my eyes quickly when I felt a wet sensation in my pants. *Did I pee in the bed?* I wondered as I groggily sat up. A tight cramp shot through my stomach. *Oh holy moly! I didn't pee in the bed!* Penny's frantic barking caught my attention. She was pawing at the door and whining, trying to get downstairs.

"Hold your horses, Penny. We'll go outside in a

minute."

I shuffled over to the dresser and pulled out a pair of pants. A spasm of pain quickly stole my breath as I struggled to pull them over my legs. Once the pain diminished, I slipped the phone into my pocket, grabbed my prepacked hospital bag, and headed for the door. As soon as I swung the door open, a wall of smoke immediately pushed me backwards. Gasping for air, I dropped to my hands and knees. I grabbed Penny's collar and crawled into the hallway. Black smoke burned my eyes, and the farther down the hall I crawled, the hotter it got. I paused at the top of the stairs as a contraction gripped my belly. *Argh!* A moan of frustration slipped out as I scooted down the stairs on my behind. I saw my entire kitchen in flames through the staircase railing and panic overwhelmed me as I struggled to breathe. Tightly holding on to Penny, we managed to make to the bottom of the stairs just as the front door flew open.

"Megs? Megan!" an unfamiliar voice shouted my name.

"Here!" I said feebly, my voice weak from the smoke

"I got you." A large frame filled the cloudy space between the stairs and the front door. Someone gently picked me up and whistled for Penny, then carried me outside. The clean air was a godsend and I struggled to breathe in as much of it as possible. The stranger took me across the street to an ambulance that had just pulled up. He set me down on the step of the ambulance and immediately, the medics set about giving me oxygen as they pulled a blanket around my shoulders. A new wave of contractions came over me and I gripped the medic's hand.

"I think I'm in labor," I wheezed.

"She's in labor. We need to get her to the hospital," The man lifted me onto the gurney as if I were lighter than air.

A woman leaned over me. "Hey doll, I'm Keri. I'm going to ask you a couple questions, okay?" She adjusted the oxygen mask over my face and hooked my finger to the pulse oximeter. "How far along are you?"

"Thirty-five weeks," I said as a cough overcame me.

"Sounds like you're almost done. You're having contractions? Do you think your water broke?" I nodded and she gestured to her partner. "Hey Manny, shut the doors alright?"

After the doors shut with a bang, she gave me a big smile. "I'm going to see if it's amniotic fluid, so just relax a bit while I push down your pants." With gloved hands, she checked with a test strip to see if there was, in fact, amniotic fluid.

"Well, Megan, your water definitely broke. Let's get you to the hospital, shall we?" she said with a smile, as if finding a woman in labor in a burning house was an everyday occurrence for her.

"I need to call my boyfriend," I said through the oxygen mask. It was difficult to speak, but Keri understood.

"We will call someone for you once we get there, but first let's take care of you."

We made it to the hospital in no time at all. Before I knew it, I was being wheeled into the bustling emergency room. I didn't see Jen, but it didn't matter. The nurses from the maternity unit whisked me right upstairs. Within minutes I was in a private delivery room. At first glance the room resembled a hotel suite with its flat screen TV and walnut décor, but I knew that the bed had stirrups and the walnut cabinets housed sterilized hardware. Once I was settled into a nifty open-back gown, and the IV was in and the monitors were hooked up, Dr. DeVaughn came in.

"Hey, Megan, let's see how we're doing." She settled onto the seat in between my legs and checked me out. "We need to keep the oxygen going. Her pulse ox is low, and get NICU. Tell them to be on standby," Dr. DeVaughn said to the nurse. "Well, Megan, I have good news and bad news. The good news is your baby is doing fine. Your daughter's heart rate is up and your contractions are consistent. We're going to have NICU on standby to check her out, because she is a little too early to be born. But she's fine. The bad news is that it's too late for an epidural. You're at eight, almost nine, centimeters dilated and 100 percent effaced. This baby is coming pretty quickly."

Fear and panic coursed through me, momentarily dulling the excruciating pain. "I need to call Shane. I need to call my mom. I can't do this by myself."

Dr. DeVaughn squeezed my hand firmly. "You're not going to be by yourself. We'll call them."

A knock on the door drew her attention away from me. Tommy's head appeared in the doorway. "Megs? Can I come in?" Without waiting for confirmation, he rushed over to the bed. "Are you okay?"

"Oh, God, Tommy. What are you doing here?" I gasped as my stomach constricted painfully.

"I heard about the fire over the PD scanner. When I got there, the ambulance was just pulling away. What can I do?"

"I need you to call Shane. Please. The baby is coming. He needs to be here. And call my mom too."

I recited Shane's number to Tommy and he went out into the hall to make the call. Dr. DeVaughn followed him out.

Ten agonizing minutes later he came back in. "Megs, he's not picking up and there's no voicemail. I just sent him a text, though. I did get in contact with your mom, but she's in West Virginia with your Aunt Amy. They are on their way now."

Another painful contraction came over me and I

gripped Tommy's hand to help me breathe through it. The need to use the bathroom soon became overwhelming. I threw the blankets off my legs and tried to sit up.

Alarmed, Tommy's eyes grew wide. "Wait, what are you doing? What do you need?"

"I need to poop. Help me up." Any sort of decorum had gone out of the window. I didn't care if he was the Pope. If I didn't go to the bathroom now, it wasn't going to be pretty.

"Whoa. Wait a minute. Let me get the doctor. I don't think you want to do that," he said, pushing the call button on the bed rail.

"Yes?" A perky voice trilled over the intercom.

"Hi. Yes...er...she needs to use the restroom," Tommy stuttered.

If I hadn't been in such agony, I would have laughed at his embarrassment. Tommy's normally olive-toned skin turned bright red.

"We'll be right there."

"Tommy, I can't wait. I need to go. Right now," I growled, desperation filling every part of my being.

"Just a minute Megan, I can almost guarantee that you don't need to use the restroom. Let me check you again," Dr. DeVaughn stated as she walked back into the room. Tommy helped me lay back down and the doctor gave me a pointed look, as if to say "I'm about to open your legs; is it okay if this man sees your hoo-ha?"

I turned to Tommy and said, "You've seen it before, but keep your eyes elsewhere." With a smirk he nodded and averted his eyes, looking everywhere but between my legs.

"Megan, you're at ten centimeters. What you're feeling is the urge to push. Don't push yet, let me finish setting up."

My eyes widened in horror. "I can't push. Not yet. Shane's not here. Mom's going to miss it. Tommy, I can't do it without them!" I said in a panic.

Just then, my cell phone rang. "Where's my cell phone? That's Shane."

Tommy went through the bag that held my smoke-filled clothes, unearthed the phone that was still lodged in my pants pocket, and handed it to me.

"Megan, what happened? I heard there was a fire. Are you all right?" Shane's voice sounded beautiful to my ears.

"Oh, God, Shane. Where the hell are you? Get here right now. I'm pushing!"

"I'm only ten minutes away from the hospital. I'm on my way, babe. I'll be right there. Hold on."

I groaned with another contraction but managed to get out, "Shane's coming."

"Good, because with the next contraction, you're going to push." Dr. DeVaughn replied, covered in hospital garb and settling into her chair.

CHAPTER 14

I︎T'S AMAZING, REALLY, how everything can change in the blink of an eye. One moment you're panicked and scared. But you fight through it, you conquer the fear, and the end result is absolute bliss.

After seven minutes of pure agonizing pain filled with pushes and screams, Katherine Louise Turner was born. At 3:49 on a Sunday morning, she weighed in at seven pounds two ounces and was perfectly healthy. After an initial checkup, the nurses allowed me to hold her in my arms. Tommy, who held my hand throughout the entire torturous process, kissed both of our foreheads and wisely left us alone to bond.

I gazed at my brown-eyed miracle in absolute awe. *How in the world can I love someone so much in such a short amount of time?* This little girl held my heart in her tiny little hand. I counted her toes and caressed her soft, brown hair, completely oblivious to the world around us.

Until I heard my name from the doorway. Shane. The nurse, Shelly, asked me if I wanted him to stay. I wanted to be a bitch. I wanted to stay mad at him for missing the birth of our daughter. But the distress and regret in his eyes had me nodding my head.

"Oh, God, Megs, I tried baby. I tried as hard as I could to get here. I'm so sorry I wasn't here with you." I nodded again, tears choking my words. Shane leaned his forehead against mine. "I'm so sorry. To both of you."

I sniffled and wiped my eyes with the thin blanket covering us. "Do you want to hold your daughter?"

The smile on his face almost made up for my disappointment. He quickly rubbed on some hand sanitizer and then reached out for her. Katie squawked in protest at being taken away from the warmth of my chest, but once Shane cradled her in his large hands, she immediately settled down.

"I can't believe how little she is," he whispered. "She looks just like you."

I quickly snapped a picture with my phone and wiped away the tears trickling down my cheek. "I can't tell yet." Nurse Shelly came over with her arms out.

"Let me take her for a few minutes. We need to

examine her more thoroughly and then we'll bring her back." Shane reluctantly passed her into the nurse's expert hands. Rubbing his goatee, he turned to me with a sad smile on his face.

"I don't know how you'll ever forgive me," he muttered, taking my hand.

"Shane, I know you tried to get here as fast as you could. No one knew it would be that quick. It sure as hell didn't go the way we planned. But yeah, I'm really frustrated. I wanted you here with me. I *needed* you here with me."

"I know, babe. When I heard about the fire—" he started.

"Oh my God," I said, interrupting him. "How much damage is there? Did we lose everything?" The night's events came crashing down on me—the smoke, the heat, the feeling of helplessness. Tears coursed down my cheeks and my heart suddenly lodged in my throat.

"Holy shit, Shane, where's Penny?" Suddenly the machines that I was hooked up to began a shrill beeping and pierced the room.

"Megs, breathe baby. Your monitors are going haywire. It's okay. Penny's fine. Cole has her at his house," Shane soothed. He gently brushed the hair away from my face. Nurse Shelly came rushing in to make sure everything was fine. After adjusting the monitor and checking my blood pressure, she gave Shane a stern look.

"I don't know what happened, but I don't want to see your heart rate go this high again," she warned. Shane nodded, holding my gaze. After she left, I grabbed his hands.

"Cole? Kate's brother? How did he know about the fire?"

"He was the one who pulled you out of the house. When he told me how close I came to losing you again, I just about lost it." Shane pressed his lips to my hands.

I rubbed my face vigorously, flustered at the quick change of events. My world felt like a game, emotions ping-ponging between happiness, fear, sorrow, and confusion.

"So Cole got me out of the house?" I asked. Shane nodded. "What happened? Do they know what caused the fire? How bad is it?"

Shane rubbed my hand. "I'm not sure. I was downtown at Ego Alley when Kate sent me a text. She found out through Cole."

"Wait. Kate's text? What about the one Tommy sent you? I mean, I know you hate the guy, but did you at least read it?" I snipped. If he hadn't returned the call back because of their petty bullshit then we were going to have even bigger issues.

Confusion crossed over Shane's face. "Uh, no. I didn't get a text. Why would he text me? Was he here?"

"He said that he tried to call you but you didn't answer so he sent you a text message. Tommy also called Mom, so she's on her way."

Annoyed, he rubbed his forehead. "Who knows? Maybe he dialed the wrong number."

"Why were you down there anyway?" I asked irritably, but our conversation was interrupted by Nurse Shelly walking in with a squawking baby in her arms. Automatically, I reached for the bundle and held her close.

"We're going to take you to your recovery room now, so just hang on tight to that little one. Are you Dad?" she asked Shane. Surprised by the question, he quickly said yes.

"Well, great. Dad, if you want to grab that bag behind you, we'll just be on our way," the perky voice chirped as she unlocked the brakes on my bed and started wheeling me out of the room.

I held Katie tightly against my chest and felt her relax as she calmed down. Her brown eyes opened and she gazed right into mine. I knew that she could only see a few inches in front of her, but my heart leapt at the thought of her recognizing me. I brushed my lips against her forehead. "It has been one hell of a night, hasn't it Katie Lou?" I whispered.

After we arrived at our private, but definitely not quiet, room, Shane dropped the bag on the chair next to the bed and put my phone on a tray. The nurses bustled around us, securing monitors and giving me a rundown of what to expect for the next twenty-four hours. Shane's eyes glazed over at the talk of breast-feeding and fecal matters. I snickered inwardly; he barely had any idea of all the fun we were about to have. Nurse Shelly took Katie from my arms and passed her over to Shane, declaring it was time for me to finally stand up. With another nurse at my side, I gingerly stood up and walked over to the bathroom.

Once I was settled back in bed and Katie was napping in her clear bassinette, the nurses brought in a set of blankets for Shane. I giggled as he tried to maneuver his large frame onto the tiny chaise lounge that served as his makeshift bed. He finally curled up on his side, his long legs hanging off the end.

"You look so uncomfortable," I managed between giggles.

"Nope, I'm fine," he replied with a yawn. I yawned in response. "Let's get some sleep, babe; it's almost six in the morning."

"Works for me." I turned the lights off using the nifty remote attached to my bed. With our room dark and quiet, the noises outside became clearer. Nurses' calls, babies' cries, and the normal early hustle and bustle of the maternity ward became our lullaby. Shane's lullaby anyway. The man could sleep through a hurricane, tornado, and a five-alarm fire without missing a snore. Even though I knew I should be exhausted, I felt like I could run a marathon. All I wanted was to hold onto Katie and count her fingers and toes again. But I knew the day would bring visitors and a nap wouldn't be in the cards, so I closed my eyes.

"Megs?" came Shane's whisper.

"Yeah?"

"Was Tommy here?"

Confused, I opened my eyes. "What do you mean, was he here? I told you he tried to call you."

Shane was quiet for a beat, then asked, "I meant, was he here when Katie was born."

Sigh. "Yes, Shane. He was here." The weariness came through loud and clear. I didn't know what he was thinking, but I knew for damn sure that he didn't want to bring up Tommy. Not now. If he gave me shit about Tommy being in the room for the birth, I would explode.

Silence. "Well, I'm glad you weren't alone. I guess if you had to be with anyone, at least you were with someone you trust."

Huh. That was unexpected.

"I love you, Megs."

"I love you too," I mumbled, closing my eyes.

CHAPTER 15

A PERSON NEVER SLEEPS WELL in a hospital, especially in the maternity ward. Nurses constantly come in to check your vitals. Or the monitors go off. Or your newborn starts crying and you have to throw your pillow at your partner to get him to wake up to bring her over to you. Sheesh. Like I said, the man could sleep through anything. After waking up momentarily confused, Katie's lusty cries finally penetrated the fog in his brain and he brought her over to me.

It took ten frustrating minutes for Katie to latch on to my breast. By the time she was feeding tears were running down my face. I winced at her first tug on my nipple, but I knew it was for the best. We had just gotten settled in when there was a knock at the door.

"Is everyone decent?" Mom called, opening the door. Pink and purple balloons floated ahead of her as she walked in with a huge smile on her face.

"Oh my goodness! I can't believe she's here!" she squealed. Mom quickly peeled off her jacket and threw it down on Shane's makeshift bed. "I got here as soon as I could. Your Aunt Amy is back at my house sleeping. You know she needs her sleep or she's a grouch. How are you feeling? Sore? Tired?" She kissed me on my forehead and gave me her special mom smile. That smile brought tears to my eyes and I quickly turned away.

"Oh, Babycakes, don't cry. I know it has been such a roller coaster for you." She sat on the edge of the bed and put her arms around me. We sat there for a minute with our heads pressed together as tears rolled down my face. She turned to Shane. "Did you speak with the fire marshal? And what happened to Penny?"

Shane shook his head. "Penny is with Kate's brother, Cole. I didn't even know the house was on fire until Kate told me. I came straight here." He checked his phone and stood up. "I'm going to run by the house now and see what's going on. Then I'll head over to Target for some clothes."

I realized that I had nothing with me, nothing for her to come home in. My purse, driver's license, insurance cards—everything was at the house. Panic rose in my chest. "Mom, what am I going to do? I don't have a license or a car seat. Everything could be gone!"

"Shhh, baby. It's all right. We'll take care of it. Try not to worry about it right now." She pulled me close as Shane put his leather jacket on. "Be safe out there, Shane. There's black ice on the roads."

"I will." He bent down and kissed my cheek, then our daughter's forehead. "I'll be back soon. Text me if you want me to bring you back anything special." I nodded and he left the room.

"Okay, it's time for me to hold my granddaughter," Mom said gleefully, rubbing her hands with excitement. She hurried to the sink and washed her hands as I dislodged my nipple from Katie's mouth.

"Megan, she looks like you," she said, cradling the quiet baby.

"That's what Shane said," I said with a smile. "She may need to burp."

Mom put Katie against her shoulder and patted her back gently as I reached for my phone. I noticed I had a voicemail message so I pressed the button to listen. My heart fell when I heard a strange man's voice on the line identify himself as the fire marshal. He told me that my side of the duplex was a total loss and my neighbor's house had suffered significant damage. He also stated that the investigation into the cause to the fire was ongoing. After saving the message so I could call him back later, I put the phone down and covered my face with my hands.

"Megan, what's wrong?" Mom asked, patting Katie's back.

"It's gone. That was the fire marshal," I said sadly. "My side is totally gone and Mr. Fader's suffered a lot of damage. We have nothing." Sobs escaped me as I rolled onto my side. I cried for the mementos I'd lost, the memories we'd made there, and the future that I'd hoped to have there with Katie. I knew it was stupid to cry, but I couldn't stop. It was my home. And now it was gone.

"Oh, Megs. I'm so sorry. But think of this: everyone is safe. You can replace pictures and dishes, but not people." Spoken like the amazing mom that she was. I nodded gratefully.

Mom stayed with me and tried to keep my spirits up. As the day wore on, more visitors filtered through. Jen and her husband, Matt, stopped by before starting their rounds as a nurse and pediatrician, respectively. Aunt Amy came with a pot of her freshly made slumgulia, which, as usual, had way too much pepper. Uncle Bob and Aunt Karen brought over a plate of cookies, and Sarah and Kyle came with bags of baby clothes. While it was great to see them all and have their support, it became overwhelming for both Katie and me. Once she started fussing late in the afternoon, Mom ushered everyone out so we could get some rest.

I had just settled her on my breast again when the door opened. Shane walked in, freshly showered and wearing a new sweatshirt. He came over, plopped the bags in the chair, and kissed us both.

"How are you?" he asked, lightly stroking Katie's cheek.

"Exhausted," I said tiredly. Nodding at his new threads, I asked, "Anything in those bags for me?"

"Yep. I picked you up some underwear, a nightgown, socks, shoes, and some sweats. I didn't get you a bra because…uh…I don't know how large those melons are now," he said with a smile. I rolled my eyes. *Of course he jokes now, but just wait until my milk comes in. He won't believe how big they get.*

"Thanks. That should work. I got a call from the fire marshal. He said the house is a total loss. Did you check it out?" I asked, adjusting my breast. Shane's eyes never left my chest. "Shane!"

"Oh! Yes, I checked out the house. It's…I don't know the words to describe it, Megs. The second floor is gone. Mr. Fader's house is pretty bad, too. My bike is destroyed; there's no salvaging it. I spoke with some people from the fire department. They said I could come back in a day or so and try to go through it and see if anything's salvageable," he said quietly.

I let out a shaky breath. "I didn't ask you, but did you check on Penny?"

"Yep. I picked up some clothes before heading to Cole's house. She's fine, hanging out with Cole's pit bull, Jax. He said that he'll keep her until we're ready to bring her home." Shane sat down at the foot of the bed. I could see the exhaustion in his face. "But I do have one piece of good news."

"Oh, yeah? What's that?" I asked wearily as Katie turned her face away from my breast and started crying. I shifted her around and tried to get her to latch on, but she struggled. Feeling frustrated, I moved her to the other side as Shane raised his voice in order to be heard over her cries.

"What?" I said, exasperated.

"I said, your car survived the fire, along with all the shower gifts!" he yelled. I felt a hard pull on my nipple and suddenly the room was quiet.

"Are you serious?" My mouth gaped open. All our shower gifts are saved? How lucky are we?

"Yep. I forgot I moved your car out of the driveway last night so I could pull my truck out. Your car is fine."

"My car is fine?" I repeated. Then a light bulb went off. "All the gifts from the shower were in the back of my car. And so was my purse."

Shane nodded. "Well, your hood has a bit of heat damage and the paint bubbled. But, all in all, it's fine. I left everything off with your Aunt Amy at your mom's house, except for a few things she thought we'd need here. Kyle was already at your mom's moving some furniture around. And I brought your wallet with me."

"Why Mom's house?" I asked, bewildered at the sudden change of events.

"Megan, I already spoke with Shane," Mom piped. "He agrees with me; you're staying at my house. You have everything you need from the shower, plus I'll be there to help you out. It makes the most sense," Mom said pointedly.

"Mom, I don't know about that." I pictured the split-level home where I grew up. The walls were paper-thin and the rooms were small. Sure, there were three bedrooms, but only one full-size bathroom. Kyle's old room was now an office and still had his baseball trophies on the wall. The basement was too drafty for the baby, so the only place that could house the three of us would be my old room. Right next to Mom's bedroom. *Yeah, that's going to be awkward.* I looked down at Katie, who had fallen asleep with my nipple in her mouth. Gently pulling free, I moved her up so she lay on my chest.

"Where else are you going to go? The only other place would be the farm, and Aunt Nancy is still fixing it up." She gave me the look that said, "Don't be silly. Do what you know is right."

"You're right. We'll stay until we figure out what to do with the house."

My mom gave me a huge smile and I just shook my head. When I truly thought about my situation, there was no place I'd rather be than home.

"Well, I'm going to leave you three be. I have a lot to do at the house before y'all move in." She kissed our cheeks and picked up her purse.

"I guess we're staying at Mom's," I said weakly. The situation wasn't ideal, but Mom was right. Where else would we go?

"You know, babe, it doesn't matter where we go. I have you and Katie; I don't need anything else," Shane whispered tenderly, stroking my cheek. He pressed his lips to mine and I felt it: despite all the drama and all the chaos in my life, Shane loved me.

CHAPTER 16

WE LEFT THE HOSPITAL THE next morning with a clean bill of health for both Katie and me along with new baby care instructions. I doubt those pages had any instructions on how to be a mom. For example, we were just about to leave the hospital when Katie decided that right then was the perfect time to explode in her diaper. Right as we're walking out the door. We had to hurry back to the maternity ward and after a couple of moments of panic, we quickly figured out how to bathe the screaming, squirming baby with the help of the nurse and a small bathtub. With that out of the way, and after Shane struggled with—and finally installed—the damn car seat, we finally made our way home. Well, to our home away from home.

I had Shane make a detour on the way to Mom's so I could survey the damage to the house. He didn't want to, but after much cajoling, he finally relented. My eyes widened in horror when Shane pulled onto Hazelnut Court. The blackened pile of brick and wood was a stark contrast to the rest of the street. Tall chain-link fencing surrounded both sides of the duplex to keep out troublemakers and looters. Shane stopped the SUV in front of Mrs. Saunders's house and we both stared at the unimaginable sight before us.

"I can't believe this. You said it was bad, but I didn't envision anything like this." I was horrified. The sheer amount of damage that the fire had caused had my heart lodged in my throat.

"I don't want to think what might have happened if Cole hadn't found you," Shane whispered. I clutched his hand tightly.

"Don't think about it. I've seen enough. Let's get going," I urged as the bile in my stomach started to churn. The very sight of the destruction made me sick. I looked over my shoulder at Katie sleeping peacefully in her seat, oblivious to the danger we'd been in. If I had my way, she'd never know.

"I told Cole that we'd stop by. I figured you'd want to see Penny," Shane said as we pulled away from the house. I tore my eyes from the burned-out frame and glanced at him.

"That sounds good. I'm sure she misses us. We'll bring her back to Mom's with us."

I never felt right when Penny was away. Ever since I picked her up from the shelter almost two years ago, we'd never really been apart. We drove a short distance before pulling up to a one-level rambler on the other side of Crofton. The house, small and comfortable, was lacking in what my real estate mother would call "curb appeal", with minimal bushes and peeling, faded blue paint. A black Jeep with purple accents was parked in the driveway along with another blue Chevy truck. I braced myself for the chilly weather and quickly zipped up my sweatshirt as Shane hopped out to get Katie. He brought her around to me, all snug in her fleece blanket. We didn't have to wait long after ringing the doorbell to hear Penny's welcome.

"Someone's happy to see us," Shane said with a smile.

I grinned. I'd missed my little mutt. The door swung open and I stepped back in surprise. The man at the door, tall and built like a tank, was none other than my brown-haired, brown-eyed rescuer from the scene of my car accident. I quickly gave Shane a questioning look before Cole said, "Hey guys, come on in. We've been waiting for you."

He opened the door wider and shooed away the two anxious dogs so we could get inside. I let Shane go in front of me, and when I walked past Cole, I asked, "Weren't you the one that helped me during my accident?"

Cole shrugged nonchalantly. "We superheroes all look the same. But, yeah, it was me."

I laughed then pulled him into a hug, surprising him.

"You saved my life twice. I don't know what to say." Tears prickled behind my eyelids. *Ugh, damn hormones. Way to go Megan, crying all over a stranger.*

Cole blushed. "It was nothing," he mumbled. His words were nearly drowned out by a squeal from behind me.

"You're here! I wasn't sure if you were coming! I'm so happy you're here," cried Kate excitedly. She threw her arms around me with such enthusiasm that she pushed me back a step. For someone so small and petite, she sure packed a punch.

"Hi. I'm glad to see you, too," I said with a chuckle. "How are you doing? You look great," I added.

Gone were the dark-brown locks with maroon highlights that I remembered from Christmas. Now her chestnut-colored locks were cut short, layered with caramel highlights. The colors made her blue eyes pop.

"I'm really great. So glad you made it. How are you? You're walking slowly. Are you in some pain?" She took the hospital-issued diaper bag from my hands and led me into a comfortable family room with neutral-toned walls, beautiful cherry floors, and brown leather couches. The outside of the house definitely did not compete with the interior.

I nodded. "I'm good. Sore, but good." Penny impatiently snuffed at my hand, begging to say hello. I bent down and vigorously rubbed her ears. "I'm so happy to see you, girl. Have you been good?"

"Yep. Her and Jax have been having a grand ole time," Cole said, patting the broad-chested, spotted pit bull next to him. Alert and friendly, I gave Jax my hand to sniff before stroking his velvety ears.

"I'm so glad to hear that—"

Kate quickly interrupted me. "Can I hold my namesake?" she asked.

Laughing, I nodded and reached for the car seat. Penny stood next to me and gently sniffed her new housemate.

As I handed her over to Kate, Penny followed my every move. Once Kate sat down on the brown patchwork chair Penny lay at her feet, not letting the baby out of her sight. As Kate oohed and aahed over Katie, Cole and Shane sat down in the pair of chocolate-colored recliners in front of the roaring fireplace. We declined Cole's offer of a drink, anxious to find out what had happened since the fire.

"My buddy is the fire marshal, and he said that even

though the fire started in the kitchen, it spread quickly, too quickly for it to be accidental. But he couldn't find an accelerant," Cole relayed.

My heart stopped. "Why would he think there was an accelerant?"

"Because of how quickly it spread. Your house was built in the eighties, sturdy with brick and good materials. Not like the crap they build now. But proving an accelerant was used would be difficult. So he's probably going to rule this accidental. Either way, he should have the final results this week."

Shane nodded. "How did you know about the fire?"

"I was on my way home and saw the smoke from Route 301. I wasn't sure if it was your house, but I didn't want to leave anything to chance. After I loaded Megan in the ambulance, I put Penny in my truck and stayed around to talk to the police," Cole replied, as if rescuing women was an everyday occurrence for him.

"Did you see anyone lingering around the house after the fire?"

"Shane, there were crowds of people and so much going on; I didn't see anything unusual. The only thing that crossed my mind at the time was to get Megan out," Cole answered.

"I owe you, so much," I said quietly.

Cole reached over and took my hand. "No, you don't. Kate asked us to look after you, but it's more than that. I'm not sure how much Shane has told you, but he's family."

I raised my eyebrow at Shane. "What don't I know?"

"Cole and I grew up together in Essex. We lived next door to each other from the time I was in diapers to when I moved down here after my folks died," Shane said sheepishly.

Confused, I glanced at Cole then turned back to Shane. "But why haven't I met him before? Why didn't you tell me this?"

"I was in a dark place. A real dark place. As much as I loved Cole and his family, I couldn't stand to be around them. It reminded me too much of what I lost. After my folks died, I moved in with my aunt and enrolled in school. Then she died two years later. I pretty much lost it then. I was eighteen and on my own. After high school I got involved with drugs and gangs and finally ended up working for Jen's dad. The only thing that saved me from offing myself was the puck and the league. I left everything behind," Shane said.

"I'm so confused. So you've known Kate for that long?" I asked.

"Yeah. After they graduated, Cole went into the SEAL program and Kate joined the FBI. It was sheer coincidence that Tommy had her partner up with me." Shane shrugged.

"Yeah, it was practically incest," Kate joked.

"Wow, that's incredible," I muttered.

"Kate was the girl you saw me with at the restaurant in Annapolis all those years ago," Shane mumbled. I inhaled sharply, remembering. When I first met Shane, I was sixteen, three years his junior. We met through our mutual best friend Jen, but I was an insecure, jealous twit. One day I found Shane with a girl (who I now knew was Kate) at a restaurant in Annapolis and flipped out into a jealous rage without letting Shane explain. My jealousy cooled our relationship until last year. *My, how things come full circle.*

"So, yeah, we're family, Megan. And we take care of our family," quipped Kate from her chair.

I giggled. "So, what else don't I know?" I asked.

"Let's see. Shane used to wet the bed until-" Cole started, but Shane slugged him in the arm. "Oh, come on! I haven't even told her any of the good ones!"

"You better not," grumbled Shane, which made me laugh even harder.

"Oh, Mom has her albums and you're in plenty of pictures. I think we have a few of your baby pictures too," teased Kate.

Shane scowled. "You're lucky you're holding my kid right now, Kate. I don't care how old you are, I can still throw your ass in the trash can."

I smacked his arm in disbelief. "You didn't!" Kate's middle finger confirmed it. "Shane, why would you throw her in the trash can?"

"Because she was a brat! Her and Charlie both. We didn't mind them at first, but they wouldn't leave us alone. We'd ride our bikes down to Turkey Point Park and they'd follow us and then tell our folks," Shane said with a huff.

"Well, if you weren't smoking up with Jimmy Carols and the Baxter boys I wouldn't have had to tattle," retorted Kate, her bright-blue eyes gleaming with mischief.

"The girls were the bane of our existence back then. Dad grounded both our asses for that. Made us go to the shipyard and clean up after the dockworkers," Cole said with a smile.

I leaned back and listened to their banter. It was nice hearing about Shane's childhood, how much of a troublemaker he was even back then. "So what's the age difference between the three of you?" I asked.

"Cole is twenty-nine, I'm twenty-six, about to turn twenty-seven on February 11, might I add—and Charlie is twenty-four. She's the baby," Kate responded. She stood up and held Katie out to Shane. "And your baby has a present for you."

Shane laughed heartily and stood to accept his stinky gift. I handed him a diaper and a package of wipes, and he made his way down the hall to what I assumed were the bedrooms. "I'll make sure she gets

Cole's bed nice and pretty," he called over his shoulder. Looking at Cole's disgusted face made me burst into gut-gripping laughter.

"Hey! I'm planning on having company later. Don't do that on my bed!" Cole retorted loudly.

"Oh my goodness, I needed that," I sighed, wiping away tears. Cole snorted while Kate studied her phone. "What's up, Kate?" I asked, noting her furrowed brow.

"What? Oh, nothing. Just a text from someone in Florida," she replied absentmindedly.

"About that, what brought you up north? I thought you were back to working in Miami," Shane questioned as he came back into the room. He handed Katie to me and sat down, pulling both of us into his arms.

Kate's eyes were guarded. "I had some time to kill."

Cole rolled his eyes at his sister. "Kate, just tell them."

Kate sighed, brushed a tendril of brown hair behind her ear, and put her phone down. "I'm on a case."

I frowned. I knew there had to be more to the story than a new lead. "Isn't that what you're supposed to do? Work on the cartel case?"

Kate shook her head. "I was pulled off the cartel case right after the holidays."

"That's fucking bullshit!" Shane's outburst startled Katie and I both.

"Really, Shane? Let the woman talk." I rolled my

eyes just as Katie started crying. Patting her bottom and gently bouncing her, I gave Shane a look that clearly said *Chill the hell out.*

"Go on," I urged her.

"Right after Christmas I went into FBI Headquarters for a check-in. Tommy was on vacation but I knew Rick would be there. So I go in, thinking everything's hunky-dory, when BAM! Special Agent in Charge Rapoles tells me that I'm temporarily 'reassigned' to Baltimore. That's fine. I'm going to miss my sexy cabana boys, but whatever. I can do more up here, right? Then he drops the bomb on me. Tells me that I'm removed from the cartel case entirely and that they want me to investigate some sort of white collar baloney completely unrelated to anything I've ever done before. I raise a big stink, I protest, beg and plead—basically anything I can do to stay on the case. But Rapoles wasn't having it. Said the order came from someone above his pay grade. I say bullshit, but what the fuck can I do? So two weeks ago, I packed up my clothes and drove back up here. I'm staying with Cole until I get my housing situation figured out."

"Yeah, we need to figure out something. You're cramping my style, kid" Cole said with a smirk.

"Please. You're not getting anything from anybody, so I'm not cramping your style, ass," she retorted with a flick of her finger.

I glanced at Shane who looked beyond pissed at these latest events.

"So, if you're off the case, how are you still getting leads? And what's going to happen now?" I asked, worried that everything we'd done so far, all the leads and tips Shane had helped track down, would be for nothing.

"Oh, I'm not giving this up. There's no way in hell I'd do that. I've been keeping up with everything thanks to Rick. Plus, I still have my contacts in Miami," she replied with confidence.

"Are you going to need me to do more?" Shane asked, ready for Kate to approve what I knew he was already planning on doing.

Kate sighed. "Unfortunately, yes. I still need your eyes and ears on the ground. At least until this case I'm working on goes to trial. I have to go dark for a while, so you can't do anything stupid, Shane."

"Dark?" I asked, concern for her—and Shane's—safety rising.

"Without direct contact. I have to go to Europe for a bit. This thing has huge implications for some prominent congressmen so they want a bunch of people on it." When I opened my mouth to ask her more, she smiled and said, "Sorry. That's all I can say."

"I'd be interested in hearing what Tommy has to say about you leaving the case," Shane muttered, rolling his eyes.

"Tommy was surprised, but he doesn't think he can do anything about it. He's trying to run the case as best he can and told me that while he hated losing me, he understood. The cartel case has grown colder and in his mind, if our resources are better used elsewhere, we have to do what we can. My position on the team hasn't gone away forever. He's still convinced that the cartel is laying low."

"Yeah, that's bullshit."

"Shane!" I said, shocked at his lack of faith. "Why would you say that?"

"Megs, I know he's your friend, but that's bullshit. You don't just express surprise at your teammate getting pulled off a case then go about your day. Not when the case is this big," Shane spat out, fury igniting behind his eyes. I pulled the baby closer, unsure of where this was heading.

"He's right, Megan. Something's not adding up. You don't put everything you have on a case then suddenly say that it doesn't matter. It's bullshit—and there's something more behind it," Cole added.

"So, what are you saying? Tommy's keeping you away from the case? Intentionally?" I demanded.

Kate shook her head. "Not necessarily. I know that every piece of evidence or lead we've given him is circumstantial at best. The leads are trickling in, and I'm making sure that whatever I get from Miami gets to Rick right away and that his team is following up on them. If something big goes down, they'll call me in."

"Then why do you need Shane?" I blurted out. If there wasn't a real need for him to go out and about gathering information for them, then why have him do it?

"Because they are still out there and we want to be one step ahead of them," Kate said bluntly. "If I can't be out there then having Shane, who used to be *in the group*, will help us get actual street intel. He won't be able to get back into the cartel, but he'll know who to talk to, who to convince to come forward."

I looked over at Cole. "And what exactly is your part in this? I mean, aside from providing a house for your sister?"

"I'll be out on the streets with Shane watching his back. I'm a former SEAL. Kate asked me for help last year after I got out of the service. I didn't want a full-time gig, but I couldn't say no. Shane's my brother. When we thought Shane was dead, I felt helpless; I didn't know what to do. I wanted you to know the truth about Kate and me, but you were dealing with Shane's death and the pregnancy..." his voice trailed off as the memories of the past few months darkened his blue eyes.

He took a swig of his beer and continued. "Kate and I—we were in shock. Not only did we fail at keeping both of you safe, but we thought we'd lost him. But I never stopped looking out for you. Like I said before, Shane is our family; he would've done the same thing if the roles were reversed. I knew that Kate would tell you eventually, but until then I had your back," Cole said solemnly. He turned to Shane. "Dude, I have to tell you, that when Kate told me you were back, that you were alive, I about passed out. It's like we got a second chance. And I promise you, I ain't letting either one of you go."

Tears welled up in my eyes. Who knew that a guy as threatening as Cole could be so sentimental?

"Thanks, bro. Now can we stop with the pansy shit?" Shane said gruffly, but with a grin. Everyone chuckled. The heartwarming moment had passed.

"So, what are you doing now that I don't need back up?" I asked Cole as I adjusted Katie.

"Megs, I'm not 100 percent certain you *don't* need back up. Kate and I are still watching over you two. Whatever goes down now, you're covered. But as for what I'm doing when I'm not watching you, I co-own a mixed martial arts training center in Gambrills called Tactical Redemption. We train fighters in boxing, Thai boxing Krav Maga, and self-defense. We also teach tactical and weapon combat to local and federal officers."

"So, if I need to learn how to kick ass, I should come to you?" I said lightly, trying to brighten the mood.

Cole snorted. "Only if you're kicking Shane's ass."

"Yeah, like she could get her leg high enough," Shane scoffed. I smacked him on the arm. My short legs were nothing to laugh at.

"How did you get involved with that?" I asked, ignoring Shane's snickering.

"When I got out of the Navy, I had no other career plans. I mean really, what other skills did I have aside from combat and handling guns? My buddy, Sketch, is an MMA fighter, and when an injury sidelined him, he had this harebrained idea to build his own center. He trained me, and after I got out he convinced me to pony up my life savings and invest it in his center. We opened two months ago and business has been good," Cole said proudly.

"And the family discount doesn't hurt either," Kate piped in.

Cole smiled. "Yeah, squirt, the fact that you train for free is a bonus, right?"

We talked with Kate and Cole for another twenty minutes or so before exhaustion came over me. Plus, it was time for me to feed Katie. So we said our good-byes, loaded Penny into the car, and drove the fifteen minutes to my mom's house. As we turned onto Manor View Road, I wistfully remembered my childhood here: riding my bike down in the woods, playing sardines in the heat of the summer nights, catching frogs in the streams behind the park. *I want that for my child.* Just as we pulled into the driveway, Mom opened the front door to the house.

"Welcome home!" she called as we got ourselves unloaded and headed inside. Penny eagerly pulled me into Mom's house and began searching for the treat jar.

"Whoa, Penny. Chill, dog. Let me get the leash off you," I said with a smile. Once free, she charged up the short flight of stairs and went straight into the kitchen.

"Hi, baby doll," Mom said, pulling me into her arms.

"Hey, Mom." She held me tightly and when she finally let go I saw tears in her eyes. "What's wrong?"

"Oh nothing. I'm just happy to have you home, that's all. I missed having you here, and now with Shane and the baby the house feels full of love," she said, wiping the tears away. *Oh Lordy. Now I know where I get my weepiness from.* I smiled at her and walked up the stairs to the main level.

My mom's house is a simple split-foyer house with the kitchen, living room, and bedrooms upstairs, and the rec room, laundry room, and family room in the basement. The other bedroom and bathroom downstairs used to belong to me, but knowing Mom it was probably full of things that she couldn't bear to throw away

"Holy shit." The living room, as small as it was, looked even smaller thanks to the piles of baby clothes and boxes of baby gear that was now filling it. Half of the things I didn't even recognize. I turned to Mom, eyes wide as saucers. "Please tell me you didn't buy out the entire baby section of Target."

Mom shook her head. "Nope. Once people heard what happened, they started bringing things over. Jen brought over bags full of Lauren's baby clothes and Zara from down the street brought the things her daughter outgrew. Your cousin, Cheryl, brought over these cases of diapers. The entire neighborhood gave something. Between this and what you got at the shower, I think you're set for a while."

Wow. The kindness and support everyone had given us overwhelmed me. Slack-jawed, I just stared at the bags of clothes, boxes of diapers, and the never-ending sea of baby stuff. "What do we do now?" I asked.

Mom gave me a gentle smile. "Now we eat dinner, then feed your baby. One thing at a time, right?"

"Norah, it smells great. I'm starved," Shane's voice carried from down the hall. Seeing his large frame holding our baby girl from the other end of the narrow hallway was such a sight. Katie's eyes were wide open; she was content in her daddy's arms.

"Good. Let's eat before she starts fussing," Mom said, taking Katie from him. As Shane and I set the table, Mom planted a loud smooch on Katie's cheek, then settled her into the baby swing that had been set up in the living room. Eating together as a family felt right.

CHAPTER 17

YEAH, THAT WHOLE NORMAL, content, happy place I mentioned? What the hell was I smoking? The next two months went by in a haze. Not a blissful, everything-is-fucking-peachy haze, but more like a sleep-deprived, over-emotional, stressed, frustrated haze. Between the rock-hard boobs, lack of sleep, lack of privacy, and lack of shower, I was a zombie. Shane tried to help as best he could, but he didn't have the proper female equipment, and I couldn't even get my own breasts to function enough to feed my own kid.

It took Shane calling Jen at three in the morning while my boobs were bared to the world, frustrated tears running down my face and Katie screaming in hunger, before I realized I had completely lost it. Mom tried to help me, bless her heart, but when Jen arrived she took one look at me and handed me a bottle of formula. Self-guilt washed over me. After reading all the stories and articles about how 'breast was best', I didn't want to admit that I had failed. Jen held me in her arms and told me that it was okay, while Shane looked on in panic. Listening to her, I realized that I was still a good mom and that I wasn't permanently damaging my child.

That wasn't our only stressor. Shane had gone through the ashes and skeleton of what was left of our home and managed to find a few things that weren't totally destroyed. After the spate of break-ins last year, which we discovered the cartel had been directly involved with, I put all my important documents and sentimental belongings in a fireproof safe under the stairs. I hadn't left anything to chance.

We received the report back from the fire marshal along with the insurance assessment. Apparently, the gas burner had been left on. I swore that I had turned it off, but then again I couldn't remember shit thanks to mommy brain. The fire was ruled accidental, but with reservations. Meaning they could open the case again if they wanted to.

Our home was considered a total loss, so we decided to take the insurance money and move on. After everything that had happened—the fire, the break-ins, the FBI raid—the thought of living there didn't sit well with me anyway. It was no longer home. After everything we'd been through together, I wanted a fresh start.

Truth be told, Mom didn't want us to move out. Granted, space was tight and the only privacy we could get was in the basement bathroom, but she was a huge asset to the both of us, especially when I went back to work six weeks after Katie was born. Depressed that I couldn't stay home longer, but knowing full well we couldn't afford for me to be a stay-at-home mom, I felt somewhat relieved that Katie was in Mom's care.

Shane, on the other hand, didn't feel depressed. Why should he? Katie was barely a week old before he was back at work, and when he wasn't at work, he was prowling the streets looking for his old drug contacts. Despite my pleas and cajoling, Shane relentlessly pursued any sort of lead connected to the cartel. We barely saw each other anymore. When he was home, he was either sleeping or eating. Forget getting up with the baby, I was surprised if he saw her for more than an hour a day. I understood that Shane had to pick up the slack while Kate was in Europe, but it was still frustrating.

Needless to say, my attitude had gone from sour to downright bitchy at times. I snapped at Mom, people in the office, even my own innocent baby. Trying to stay strong, trying to stay above the fray, had worn me thin. Valentine's Day came and went with barely a mention;

all I received was a last minute bouquet of wilted roses from the gas station. Of course, I tried to downplay the holiday, but it being the first Valentine's Day for us as a couple, I couldn't help but feel disappointed when he walked in at eleven thirty that night. Katie had been up crying because of gas and my nerves were shot. Exhausted, I just handed him the card I had made for him from Katie and the gift-wrapped Fossil watch that I'd had engraved, and went into the bedroom. Shane felt horrible, which made me feel even worse. I hadn't been the most pleasant person to be around either, so I knew I was giving off mixed signals. I'm not sure what pissed me off more, the fact that the flowers were so obviously an afterthought or that he hadn't even bothered to come home until he thought I was in bed.

After more than a month of silent treatments, short tempers, curt responses, and icy glares, I was done. I couldn't stand to be the bitch anymore. So I pushed past the feelings of disappointment and loneliness and moved forward. With everything that was going on, it had been easy to lose sight of what was important. Relationships are something you constantly have to work on—so Jen told me when I called her in tears.

That mantra ran through my head as I prepared a dinner for Shane to try to bridge the distance that had grown between us, to reconnect without the anxiety and stress of having a newborn crying ten feet away.

Everything was on track and going according to plan. Mom took Katie over to Aunt Nancy's for the weekend and I sent Shane a text telling him that dinner was at six o'clock and that we were child-free for the weekend. With an hour to spare, I quickly showered and shaved my legs. Although it had only been eight weeks since we were last intimate, I felt like I was prepping for my first time. All the books said that the first time after having a baby is somewhat awkward and potentially uncomfortable, but I figured a romantic night together was exactly what we needed to relieve the tension in our relationship.

Forgoing panties and wearing my best push-up bra, I pulled out my little black dress from its hiding place in the back of Mom's closet. After struggling with the zipper, I realized I hadn't quite yet lost all the baby weight. Sighing in frustration, I slipped into a stretchy, cotton, navy-blue wrap dress that was more forgiving. I dried my hair, applied my makeup, and checked the time. *Quarter to six. Perfect.* I hurried into the kitchen, pulled dinner out of the oven, and lit the candles. I sat down and waited for the roar of his truck.

My hope that I could bring freshness into the relationship diminished as time ticked by and his favorite penne rustica grew cold. My phone calls went unanswered, but I finally received a text response saying that he was running late and would be home soon—at eight o'clock. An hour and half later, my phone lit up with a message. My hope deflated again when I saw it was from Jen.

Don't forget that Jason's going away party is tonight at Double J's. We're on our way. See you there?

I had totally forgotten about Jason Russo's party. He had been a good friend since high school and was one of the owners of Double J's, the local bar. Baseball was in his blood and he had finally gotten called up to the major leagues; he would be training with the Tampa Bay Rays and starting on Monday. I sat for a minute and debated with myself. Part of me—the wistful, hopeful, romantic part—wanted to stay home and wait. The other part— the part that was growing more and more pissed as each second ticked by—wanted to say fuck it and go.

I quickly sent off a test text message to see how he'd respond: "Are you on your way?"

Five minutes later: "I'm in the middle of something. Will call soon."

"Fuck it," I growled as I texted him back. "Don't bother. I'm going out."

I threw my phone onto the table. There was no point in waiting for his call. If anything, it would probably be best that I *not* answer his call if and when it came, especially with the heated anger I was feeling. At what point would I stop being an afterthought? After putting away the food, I headed down the hall to change. After putting on panties, jeans, and a V-neck cream-colored sweater, I quickly locked up the house and hopped into my car.

When I got to Double J's, I was greeted by many familiar faces. Everyone in town was there to say good-bye to the local celebrity. Voices struggled to be heard over the sounds of Southern Edge, a local band that had been getting a lot of radio play recently. Josh, Jason's brother and co-owner of Double J's, maintained his post by the kitchen, surveying the crowd and making sure everyone was happy while Noah, their cousin, proved his skills behind the bar. And, of course, the guest of honor held court at the center table.

"Hey, Megs," Jason said, noticing my wave. Standing at six foot even, I barely made it up to his chest so he had to bend over to hug me.

"I'm so happy for you!" I cried with a smile on my face.

"Thanks. It's good to see you. I'm glad you could come out. Where's Shane?" he asked, gazing around the room.

"Don't know," I said with a shrug, ignoring Jason's raised eyebrow. "When do you roll out? You have to report on Monday, right?" I changed the subject. Knowing Jason, he'd press until he got answers.

He gave me a look that said he knew what I was doing, but he let it slide. "I drive down tomorrow and have to check in Tuesday morning," he replied, leaning in so I could hear him.

"Is Ashley going with you?" I asked loudly, mentioning his longtime girlfriend.

"You mean is my fiancée going with me?"

That sly dog. He's been holding out on me. Well, hell, the world could have ended last week and I'd still be wandering around, asking what happened. That's how far removed I was from the rest of the world.

"About freaking time! How long has it been? Three, four years now? Congratulations!" I said, giving him another hug.

"It's been five years. She's been down there for a month now, since winter semester started. I had to settle up a few things here with Josh and Noah before heading down. Noah bought half of each of our shares. He's now the third co-owner," he said with a smile. Knowing their family history, I wasn't surprised that having Noah on board made Jason feel better about leaving the place.

I felt guilty taking him away from the celebration, so I gave him another hug good-bye, promised to text him often, and then went in search of Jen and Matt, finally spotting them at our normal corner booth

"Hey guys!" I called over the sound of Southern Edge's latest single. With a heavy guitar riff in the background, I settled myself next to my best friend.

"I'm so glad you came out!" Jen said, giving me a

hug. I leaned over her and kissed Matt's cheek.

"Yeah, I was due for a good time." I managed to get the server's attention and ordered a hard apple cider.

"Where's Shane? Is he here with you?" I gave her a look, and she immediately took the hint.

"What happened?" she asked gently.

I shook my head and took a long sip of the crisp cider. *God, that tastes amazing.*

"Megs?" Jen tried again, touching my arm. After draining half the bottle, I finally looked at her.

"I have no idea. I texted him and all I got back was, in the middle of something, will call later. So instead of waiting for him, like I've been doing for the past few months, I'm here, having fun." The sadness in her eyes ignited the flame of rage that had been smoldering in my stomach. *Fuck this. I don't want her damn pity.* "Don't worry about it. We're fine. Just thought we could do something fun tonight since Mom has Katie, but apparently he has other plans."

I finished off the rest of the cider and started looking around for the server, but decided that going to the bar would be faster. "I'm getting another drink. Want one?" They both shook their heads. I made my way to the bar where Noah and Fallon, my other favorite bartender, were serving drinks as fast as they could.

"Hey, Noah. Can I get a cider?" I asked once I finally grabbed his attention. Noah Russo, looking gorgeous as ever with his lean, muscular build and chocolate-brown eyes with thick, dark lashes, gave me a sexy grin.

"For you, good lookin', anything," he said with his country drawl. Noah popped the top of my favorite brew and set it in front of me. I protested when he wouldn't accept my cash. "Nah, Megs. It's compliments from the man at the end of the bar."

Surprised, I looked in the direction he pointed and locked eyes with Tommy. Thanking Noah, I meandered my way through the crowd toward Tommy, curious as to why he was here. This was a private party and I'm pretty sure he wasn't close with Jason.

I walked down to the end of the bar. "Thanks for the drink," I said, giving Tommy a hug.

"You're welcome," he said with a smile. "You're looking good."

"You're looking pretty decent yourself. Haven't seen you out of your suit in a while." Dressed in dark jeans and a black button-down shirt, Tommy looked more relaxed than I'd seen him in a long time.

Chuckling, Tommy drew on his longneck beer. "Yeah, it's been a while. I finally have a night off. How's the baby? Everything going okay?"

"She's great. Everything else is good." *Except for Shane ditching me tonight.* "Are you here with Jessica?" I asked, taking a huge gulp of my drink.

Tommy shook his head. "She had to work tonight.

Where's your man?"

I shrugged. The alcohol was beginning to hit my system and my resentment toward Shane was slowly fading away. It wasn't as if I didn't care where Shane was, but I could go out and have a good time without him. I ignored Tommy's questioning look and moved past the elephant in the room.

"So, I didn't know you were close with Jason."

It was Tommy's turn to shrug. "I make it my business to get to know the local establishments, to build relationships. If any shit goes down, it makes both our lives easier. Besides, they have kick-ass wings."

I nodded. I guess that made sense. "How's it going at work? How's the case on the cartel coming?" I asked, my voice low in his ear. Tommy looked taken aback for a second, but quickly recovered.

"The case is coming along, but there's not much going on right now. Everyone's pretty much scattered in the wind." He drank more of his beer.

Huh. Then why is Shane spending so much time working on it?

I opened my mouth to reply, but Southern Edge broke into a cover of "Funky Cold Medina", and my body started moving on its own. A cheer went up in the room and the energy became contagious.

"Come on, let's dance," I pleaded, putting my empty bottle on the bar.

"You know I don't dance," Tommy said with a laugh. "I'll be right back. I need to make a phone call."

"You big pussy," I teased, turning toward the dance floor. Jen grabbed my hand and led me into the mob that was gyrating and dancing to the beat. We stayed on the dance floor for a while. When the band took a break, Jen and I headed to the bar, determined to quench our thirst. I chugged another crisp apple cider like it was water.

"Hey, let's do shots," I exclaimed after my beer was finished. Apparently, I said it loud enough and a cheer erupted from the people around us. "Noah, can we get some Washington Apple shots?" Shaking his head with laughter, he set up the shot glasses and started pouring the Crown Royal.

"Oh, Lordy," Jen said with a smile. Noah handed us the glasses full of whiskey, Apple Pucker, and cranberry juice.

"Here's to the men who make us crazy and to us for putting up with their shit," I called, holding the glass with unsteady hands.

"I'll drink to that." We clinked glasses and drank the tart, sweet mixture in one swallow. I slammed down the glass and called for another. Jen refused, shaking her head.

"What? Come on, Jen!" Noah put fresh shots down in front of us.

"Nope, I'm good. Lauren may be at my mom's, but I do have to pick her up at some point." Jen laughed, mentioning her four-year-old daughter.

"Hell then, no use wasting a good drink." I took her shot and drank it quickly. Jen's look of concern bothered me.

"What?" I couldn't help sounding annoyed. "I'm just trying to have a little fun. Put some of the drama behind me, let loose, ya know?"

"Yeah, I know. Just haven't seen you drink like this in a while," she said, watching me order another cider.

"Well, yeah, it's been forever since I've gotten to go out and just be *me*. I've had a dead boyfriend, a cartel chasing me, a baby, a house fire, and now my boyfriend is off doing God knows what. Plus, I haven't gotten laid in like, *forever*. Shit, I deserve this." *Does my voice sound funny?* I giggled, then tried to put on a serious face.

"You're right, you deserve a good time. But don't you think you're over doing it?" I rolled my eyes at her and stuck out my tongue. Southern Edge came back to the stage, and immediately started playing "Pour Some Sugar on Me".

"Come on, let's dance!" I didn't give her a chance to answer but pulled her away from the bar. We danced for a few more songs until the ballad Southern Edge is most known for, "Losing You", came over the speakers. Jen found Matt, who would only dance to slow songs, and left me in the middle of the dance floor alone. *Awkward.* Tears of self-pity stung behind my eyes as I glanced around at all the couples gazing adoringly into each other's eyes. *Ugh. I will NOT be the drunk crier,* I thought with resolve, walking back to the bar. Knowing I'd better sober up, I asked Noah for a soda and my tab.

"I got you," Tommy said behind me. I quickly turned around at the sound of his voice and my feet got tangled up. I lost my balance and fell right into his arms. "Shoot, now I really got you."

"Thanks, Tommy," I grabbed the bar to pull myself out of his embrace and a giggle escaped me. "Whoops."

"Oh hell. You're drunk," Tommy muttered.

"Am not!" I cried indignantly. *Okay, maybe a smidge.*

"You're not driving home like this," he retorted angrily. *What the fuck? Why was he pissed?*

"No shit, Sherlock. I'll get a ride with Jen," I snapped, pulling my arm away.

Suddenly, I heard Shane's voice. "Fuck that. I'm taking your ass home."

Oh, shit, I thought. The anger in his tone startled me. Wincing, I turned around. Fury danced in his eyes. *Remember you're pissed at him,* I told myself. I snuck a glance at Tommy, who was smirking, and steeled myself against Shane's furious stare.

"What are you doing here, Shane?" I crossed my arms and tried to give him the death stare, but only erupted in giggles.

"Oh, for fuck's sake. You're fucking hammered," Shane rolled his eyes and made a grab for my arm. Instinctively, I pulled away.

"So what? I'm having a good time."

"Shane, why don't I—" Tommy interjected, but Shane cut him off.

"Tommy, shut up. You're not involved in this," Shane warned.

"The hell I'm not. I'm looking out for her, making sure she's okay. What were you thinking, letting her drink like this by herself?" Tommy shot back. *Oh shit, this isn't good.* Given the history between these guys, I knew I needed to step in.

"Hey, both of you shut up. Jen and Matt are here; they'll take me home," I retorted.

"Megan, don't be ridiculous—" Shane started, reaching for my hand.

"No. Shut your damn mouth. I'm so fucking pissed at you right now. The one night we're baby-free and you're too busy to hang out with me? You don't call when you're running late? I had dinner on the table, waiting for you. *Again*, Shane. You're never home anymore. Where the hell were you?" I snapped.

Tommy leaned against the bar with a smirk across his face, as if he was enjoying our drama. Shane opened his mouth to speak, but nothing came out. The lack of excuses or reasoning sent my temper through the roof. *I don't need this bullshit. If he can't tell me what he was doing and can't bother to call me then screw him.* I just shook my head.

"Fuck it," I said softly. Even over the din in the bar, I knew he heard what I said. I turned on my heel and headed toward the corner booth where Jen and Matt were waiting.

"Dammit, Megan, wait!" Shane's voice bellowed behind me. Fighting back the tears, I stopped. I was tired of being taken for granted. Sulking, I turned around with my arms crossed and waited for his apology.

"Look Megan, it's been—" Shane started. But an all too familiar pop radiated throughout the room, startling the crowd. Murmurs and low chatter momentarily sidetracked the crowd from its dancing and boozing.

"What the hell was that?" I asked, my eyes widening, though I knew the answer even through my drunken haze. Shane gripped my hand tightly, his body tense, as he scanned the room. His eyes locked with Tommy, who gave a sharp nod. They knew exactly what that sound was. With everything we'd been through in the past year, and despite their hatred for each other, Tommy and Shane's main focus was my safety. Tommy spoke into his earpiece and requested backup. He reached underneath his shirt for his gun and moved toward the back hallway. Shane turned to me with urgency.

"You need to get out of here," he said, his voice low in my ear. I opened my mouth to speak, but three loud shots and then a shrill scream silenced me. "Go!" he said, pushing me to the door. Panic rippled through the club and quickly reached the height of hysteria. Shane reached into his back waistband, pulled out a silver gun, and raced back to Tommy. I shouted his name but it was lost in the sounds of chaos.

Matt and Jen appeared next to me and grabbed my wrist. "Let's go, Megan!" she cried, yanking me toward the door. Swept up in the wave of confusion and terror, the crowd rushed the exits, with Jason and Josh helping those who had fallen. Once outside, we saw the police, who were moving people across the parking lot to the sidewalk in front of the adjacent stores. More police cars pulled into the shopping center and blocked the entrances to keep people from leaving.

"What the hell is going on? This never happens around here," Jen asked, gasping to catch her breath. Matt rubbed her back absentmindedly. People huddled for warmth against the crisp March air in front of the darkened nail salon and closed eateries. I ignored the question, searching each face and body in search of Shane.

"They haven't come out yet. Where are they?" I wondered aloud. Fear for Shane's and Tommy's lives was twisting my body into knots. *Any minute. They'll come out any minute now.* Suddenly, two more shots rang out and screams echoed through the night air.

CHAPTER 18

"S HANE!" I SCREAMED, lunging forward. Matt's broad arms grabbed me before I could get any farther. "Let me go! Shane's in there!"

"Megs, you can't go in there. The cops and Tommy are with him. He's safe," Matt soothed. Tears coursed down my cheeks as I sobbed in Matt's arms, fearing the worst.

We waited for what seemed like forever. My heart dropped as the SWAT van pulled in next to Double J's. I spied Kyle's buddies and fellow officers working the crowd, and they gestured that they'd come over shortly. Finally, they made their way over to us with grim looks on their faces.

"Where's Shane?" I demanded, wiping away my

tears. Officer Fiedler, a friend of mine since middle school, heaved a big sigh. His face drawn in a frown, he uttered the words that tore through me.

"You know we aren't allowed to talk about this, but you deserve to know. I don't want to alarm you, but Shane's been injured, Megs, and there's one fatality. But we can't get to them. The shooter is still inside and he has a hostage." My knees buckled. Luckily Jen and Matt were there to hold me up.

"How bad?" I asked.

Knowing they shouldn't go into detail but sensing my fear and panic, Officer Farr offered what he knew. "We're not sure. We've been speaking with Tommy on his cell phone and he said that Shane was shot in the chest. The hostage negotiator is talking with the shooter now, trying to talk him into allowing the EMTs access to him, but so far the asshole's not budging. We have a sniper in place now. As soon as we get the bastard down, we'll be able to assess Shane."

Fresh tears made their way down my cheeks as I thanked my friends. Jen, Matt, and I waited with trepidation as time went by. The shopping center became a circus as the media swooped into this normally quiet riverside town where the biggest news events are usually car accidents and random juvenile antics. Hostage situations and bar shootings weren't part of the vernacular of Anne Arundel County as a whole, much less Edgewater.

Minutes ticked by and my nerves were shot. Finally, a single, loud pop rang out. *"Go, Go, Go!"* sounded through the radio. EMTs and fellow officers rushed into the bar. I pulled out of Jen's arms and hurried over to the entrance, only to have an officer deny me entry.

"That's my boyfriend in there! I need to see him!" I demanded, my normal respect for law enforcement in shreds.

"Hey, Doug, she's with me." Tommy's voice came from the back of the bar. Seeing my opportunity, I pushed Doug's arm aside and ran into the bar, meeting Tommy halfway.

His arms encircled my waist as I tried to get by. A huddled group of medics worked feverishly on a still body lying on the floor. I couldn't see the face, but my heart knew. I struggled against Tommy to get to Shane.

"I need him, Tommy. I need to see if he's all right. Please, Tommy." I begged and pleaded, but his arms tightened around me.

"Megs, let them work on him. He lost a lot of blood." Tommy said roughly.

"Clear!" shouted an EMT. I watched in absolute horror as they placed the defibrillator on his chest. "We got a reading. Let's get him out of here." Moving quickly, they loaded Shane onto the gurney and started for the door.

"I'm going with him," I stated, daring anyone to object. I ran for the booth where we had sat earlier. I grabbed the purses and jackets, then dashed after the EMTs.

"I'll meet you there," Tommy called from behind me. I didn't bother to answer. My only objective was to make sure Shane was okay. Jen and Matt waited by the door, anxious for an update. I handed off their belongings and quickly told them what I knew.

"I'll call you guys once I find out anything," I added, getting into the ambulance. Looking at Shane scared me and I wanted to cry. Pale and still, the only way I knew he was alive was the barely visible rise and fall of his chest. I tuned out the noises and the chatter, the beeps and monitors. My sole focus was him. I desperately wanted to hold his hand, to make sure he knew I was there, but I stayed in my seat, not wanting to get in anyone's way.

Within ten minutes we arrived at the medical center emergency room. Jumping out of the ambulance, I followed the EMTs as they wheeled Shane into the ER, but I was prevented from going with him.

"Miss, you have to stay here," a no-nonsense nurse said to me. Despite my pleas and angry outbursts, she wouldn't relent. I resigned myself to the sterile, uncomfortable waiting room, growing more frustrated as time clicked by. I filled out paperwork for him, answering only the questions I knew and putting my name down as his spouse. After thirty minutes, a doctor came out to talk to me. He told me that Shane's lung had collapsed and that he needed surgery to remove the bullet from his chest, but the good news was that he was alive. I finally allowed myself a bit of relief, but I knew I wouldn't feel better until he was out of surgery. I texted Adrian, Jen, and Mom once I had the piece of good news, then sat down to wait.

"Hey, Megs." Tommy walked over and sat down beside me. "How's Shane?"

I rubbed my face tiredly. "His lung collapsed and he's in surgery right now." His arm came around my shoulders and pulled me into him. I closed my eyes and sighed. We sat like that for a few minutes before I looked up at him. His face was haggard. I felt bad; I had momentarily forgotten that Tommy had been in danger too.

"Hey, how are you doing? You okay?" I asked softly, squeezing his hand.

Tommy gave me a grim smile. "Yeah, I'm cool."

"What happened in there tonight?" I knew if he said anything it would break all sorts of protocols and rules, but I needed to make sense of what happened.

Tommy exhaled slowly. "It was a drug deal gone bad. From what we can figure out, the shooter, Diego Constantine, was dealing drugs to an eighteen-year-old waitress and was caught in the act by an off-duty cop, Mark Sinclair. That was the first shot we heard. We think he panicked when Mark walked back there; killing him was a knee jerk reaction. When Shane and I got there, he was freaking out, screaming at the waitress. Then he grabbed her and put the gun to her head."

I gasped. "Is she okay?"

"She's dead. Shane went for her, but Diego shot him, and then her," he said gravely. He bent over and rested his chin in his hands. "Megs, I tried to get to them both, but Diego had the upper hand. I couldn't move."

It was my turn to comfort him. Tommy took each loss of life hard; he felt like he failed the victims. I shook my head at the senseless tragedies that had taken place. Violence seemed to follow me. Was I the reason behind it? Was the cartel targeting everyone I love? What the hell had I done, bringing a child into this world? Was this going to be her life, too? When was this going to end? Anxious questions whirled in my mind, making me rethink everything. *Maybe coming home wasn't the best idea.*

Another hour passed as Tommy and I silently sat in the cold, chaotic room. I tuned out the wails of family members, the drunkards who lurched and stumbled around, and the children crying because they were ill. My only concern was Shane. At two in the morning, the doctor came walking through the automatic double doors and we stood to meet him.

"Your husband is a lucky man, Mrs. Turner. The surgery went well and he's in recovery. The collapsed lung was repaired and the bullet didn't do any major damage beyond that. He's in the ICU right now, but if things go well, he should be able to go home in a few days."

Relief coursed through my body. I pulled the doctor into a tight hug. "Thank you so much," I whispered, brushing away the tears. "Can I see him?" The doctor nodded and led us to his room.

"I'll wait out here," Tommy muttered.

I walked with the doctor though the maze of corridors that led to Shane's room. The only sounds were the heart monitor and the sound of the ventilation machine. His ashen face looked peaceful as he lay there among the wires.

"The detectives came to ask questions, but I sent them away. Shane's in no shape to talk to them and he needs his rest. And so do you," the doctor gently chided. "I'll allow a few minutes, but then I want you to go home." He made a notation on Shane's chart and left the room.

Pulling a chair up to the bed, I gently took his hand and put it up to my lips. He slowly woke, and I had never been more grateful to see those hazel eyes.

"Hey, baby. How are you feeling?" I whispered,

brushing my fingers against his scruffy chin.

Shane licked his dry lips. "Like I was shot," he groaned dryly. I picked up the cup of water on his bedside and held the straw to his lips. He eagerly drank.

"The doctor says that you're going to be fine. You just need to hang out here for a few days." Shane nodded, his eyes closing. Then he snapped them open.

"What happened to Diego?"

I sighed. "The sniper got him. The waitress, the off-duty cop, they are both dead."

"Fuck," he groaned.

"I know."

"They weren't supposed to be there."

"Yeah, I guess it was the wrong place, wrong time for the three of you."

"No. Not that," he said, frustrated. "Diego had ties to the Cruz Cartel. I used to run with him when I was part of the group. I ran into him about a month ago down at Smokey's Deli. We got to talking. For a while he was gung ho. The crew was his life; he lived and breathed that shit. After I left, got caught, whatever, he realized that maybe being with them wasn't such a good thing. Especially now that he had a new baby boy and a girl down in Virginia Beach that he wanted to be with. Diego's a good guy; he was tired of the life and already out on parole. He didn't want to go back to the cell and was scared out of his mind. But he knew what had happened to me. He was going back and forth on bailing out. We'd talk a couple of times a week. I kept telling him that once we got the cartel dismantled, we would be safe. But he kept saying the he doesn't trust anyone and there's no loyalty anymore. I almost had him convinced to meet with Rick."

"What happened? Did you meet him at Double J's?"

"No, I met him over at the park on Patuxent River Road. We talked for a while and Rick was going to meet us there. But Diego had a deal to make, so we drove up to the bar. He went to go do his thing and that's when I saw you."

"Tommy said that Diego shot Mark because Mark was undercover," I informed Shane, giving him another sip of his water.

"That would explain why Diego looked deranged. Obviously he didn't know Mark was undercover, or we wouldn't have gone there."

"That's probably why he shot you too," I surmised. Shane looked confused.

"Megs, I have no idea who shot me. At one point I thought there was someone else back there, but who the hell knows. When I showed up, Tommy had his gun drawn on Diego, Diego had his gun on the waitress, and then he started screaming at me that I played him. Mark was on the ground, bleeding out of his head. It was tense as hell and everyone was on edge."

There was a knock at the door. "Mrs. Turner, your husband needs his rest," the nurse reminded me sternly. I sighed, stood, and brushed my lips against his.

"Mrs. Turner?" he asked with a grin.

"Hey, it worked for you when I was in the hospital. Just another technicality," I joked. "She's right, though. I need to go. But I'll be back tomorrow morning," I said, pulling on my jacket.

"You're going to nurse me back to health? You know that requires a naughty nurse uniform, right?" he smirked, wiggling his eyebrows suggestively. *Seriously? The man has been shot and he's already thinking about getting some action?* I groaned and swatted his arm lightly.

"If that's what it takes to get you better and home, fine. I'll pick one up tomorrow," I joked, rolling my eyes. "Get some sleep. I love you."

"I love you, too."

By the time I got back to the waiting room, exhaustion had kicked in and my body felt like it was dragging. I was ready to drop. Hell, even the hard-as-stone chairs looked mighty comfortable by that point. Even Kyle thought so, I thought, finding him snoring away in the corner. *Where the hell did Tommy go?*

"Hey, wake up," I said loudly, kicking the leg of his chair. Kyle woke with a start.

"Gee, thanks for that," he said snidely, stretching his long legs.

"Where's Tommy?"

"I came in and he was on his way out the door. He had to go write up what happened so I'm taking you back to Mom's. We'll get your car tomorrow." He yawned loudly.

Good. I didn't want to have to deal with Tommy's questioning. "Let's go. I'm beat," I replied.

"Yeah, I can see that, grump ass." I smacked him hard on the upper arm, which he just brushed off.

"How is he?" Kyle asked once we were in his truck. With the heater running full blast, I felt my bones begin to thaw.

"His lung collapsed, but other than that, he's good. Bullet didn't do any major damage and he should be out in a few days."

"That's good news. Did he say what happened?" Kyle asked, making the left onto Route 450. I relayed what Shane had told me and had finished by the time we reached Patuxent River Road.

Kyle whistled. "Damn, Megan. What the hell was he doing with Diego? I thought he would stay clear of that mess."

I rubbed my eyes as a yawn escaped. "I don't know. I truly don't know. He says it is because of what they did to Eric, to him, and what they did to us. I don't know if he's trying to prove something or if it's purely revenge, but whatever it is, I'm tired of it."

Kyle slowed the truck down as he went around a sharp curve. The twisty, windy road ran through the hills and dense woods of Davidsonville and wasn't the most driver friendly. Blind curves, wet roads, and skittish wildlife were the frequent causes of many accidents in this area, regardless of the time of day.

"Kyle, look out!" I cried as a silver sedan pulled out in front of us from a blind curve.

Kyle slammed on his brakes, almost hitting the car. "What the fuck?" Kyle shouted. The silver sedan sped off, oblivious to the fact that we had almost collided. "Goddamned mother—Are you okay?"

I let out a shaky breath as he slowly pressed on the gas. "Yeah." I glanced over as we passed the entrance to Davidsonville Park. A slight wisp of smoke caught my attention. "Kyle, do you see that? I think I saw smoke coming from back there."

Cursing under his breath, he pulled a U-turn at Double Gate Road. "Fuck. I need to check it out." Kyle pulled into the dark athletic park and scanned the fields as we slowly drove down the road. "Keep your eyes open. Let me know if you see anything," he muttered.

"It's pitch black; I can't see my hand in front of my face," I replied, looking out my window.

"Hold up. Is that smoke?" Kyle peered ahead and accelerated. The truck surged forward and ran over the speed bump as if it were a crack in the road. In the back corner of the park, next to a brick building, was a large SUV on fire. "Shit."

Before we were even parked he dialed dispatch. "Yeah, this is Officer Kyle Connors, ID Number P37262. Want to report a vehicle fire at Davidsonville Park, Patuxent River Road. Victims unknown. I also want to get out an APB on a silver Cadillac CTS that left the scene not more than five minutes ago, heading south on Patuxent River Road. Plate number is X-ray, Tango, Foxtrot, number one, number four, number seven." He threw the truck in park. "Yeah, I'll meet him here." He flipped off the phone and reached behind the seat. "Stay here!" he ordered as he pulled out a small fire extinguisher.

I watched in fear as my younger brother did his best to fight the blaze with his extinguisher, but the small canister lost the battle against the flame-engulfed vehicle. He threw the canister aside and rushed back to the truck. "I couldn't get close enough to do anything and I sure as hell can't see if anyone is inside.

Five minutes later the sirens of Crofton's fire department echoed through the night, followed by several police cars. Kyle and I stood back, letting the professionals do what they did best while answering questions from the police. We had just finished up when a shout was heard over the loud engines of the trucks.

"We have a body!"

Several of the officers, including Kyle, ran over to the smoldering vehicle. I climbed back into the truck and waited. Seeing a burned-out corpse didn't rank high on my list of things I'd like to do.

Ten minutes later Kyle walked over to me, his face grim. He climbed into the truck, rubbed his face, and stared at the officers working at the scene.

"Kyle?" I asked gently, not knowing what to say.

"We know her. I mean, we *knew* her," Kyle said softly.

"Who was it, Kyle?" My heart leapt into my throat and I grabbed his hand.

"Rachel Morrison."

The name of Adrian's former girlfriend brought tears to my eyes and my heart sank.

"Are you sure it was her?" I demanded, waiting for a glimmer of hope.

Kyle nodded. "Yeah. Her wallet was found a good ways outside the car, as if whoever did this wanted the police to know it was her."

"Oh, no." I breathed through the sudden nausea billowing up inside me.

"What happened?" I asked shakily. Kyle draped his arm around my shoulder and sighed. "Kyle, what the fuck happened?" I demanded.

"I don't know, Megs. Detective Ford is taking lead. He's one of the best in the state, if not the region. I'm going to take you home, then I'm coming back to see if

I can be of any assistance." He turned the ignition key and put the truck in reverse. We slowly made our way past the roaming officers and pulled back onto the street.

Rachel, the sister of slain Eric Morrison, who was one of Shane's best friends and a member of the Cruz Cartel. Eric died in a drug deal last year. His death was the catalyst for Shane's placement in the safe house. Rachel was a schoolteacher, and Adrian's long-time love. Once Rachel heard how Eric had died, and that Adrian knew about the cartel, she left him and never saw him again. *Another life lost at the hands of the cartel.* I had no proof whatsoever that the cartel was behind this, but the knots in my gut told me they were.

I let the tears fall freely as Kyle pulled into Mom's driveway. Dark and quiet, I looked at the empty house with apprehension. After everything that had happened in the last six hours, I really didn't want to be in the house by myself.

"Why don't you stay with us? You don't need to stay here," offered Kyle, seeing my hesitation.

I shook my head and stared at the dark house. "I know. I just want to sleep in my own bed." The day's drama weighed heavily on my shoulders. *Pull up your big girl undies and get in there,* I told myself. But the seatbelt didn't magically come off and I couldn't budge.

Kyle got out of the truck. "At least let me check out the house. Stay here." I rolled my eyes at his command.

Yeah, buddy. I ain't going anywhere.

Each window lit up as Kyle checked the rooms. After five minutes, he poked his head out. "It's clear," he called. The second he said those words, my ass was out of the truck and into the house so fast it was as if the boogeyman himself were chasing me. Once inside, and behind the safety of the locked doors, I found myself able to breathe.

"You better get going," I told my brother as I poured myself a glass of milk. "Sarah's going to be worried." I knew Kyle's wife, and my old college roommate, understood the downfalls of marrying a cop, but I hated to have her worry unnecessarily.

"I called her when I came in. She insisted that I stay here tonight," he said, stretching his legs out on the couch.

"So you're not going back?"

Kyle adjusted the floral throw pillow. "Nope. I have orders from She Who Must Be Obeyed to stay right here."

I groaned. "I'll be fine. Go home to your wife," I protested, sitting on the brown chair across from him. Penny came over and laid her head on my lap, sensing my need for comfort.

"Your friend threatened to withhold any marital benefits if I listened to you. And I love my marital benefits," Kyle smirked. He closed his eyes. "Just grab me a blanket from Mom's room and you won't even know I'm here."

I obliged. Soft snores were already radiating from the couch when I placed Mom's navy fleece blanket over Kyle's lanky form. I set the burglar alarm and with Penny and Mom's fourteen-year-old bichon, Micki, padding behind me, I headed down the hall to my cramped bedroom. Overflowing laundry baskets held our clothes and Katie's bassinet was squeezed into the corner next to the full-sized bed that Shane and I shared. Shedding my clothes and dropping them on the floor, I collapsed onto the bed in tears and cried myself to sleep.

CHAPTER 19

S HANE WAS RELEASED from the hospital a week later. Once released, he demanded to be brought up to speed on the standing of the Cruz Cartel. Despite Tommy's earlier protests that the cartel members had dispersed, new evidence from Kate's sources in Miami had brought to light that they had become more active in Florida. We learned from Kate and Rick that the cartel was not only back in business, but also was gaining serious momentum. Kate was brought back to the case, flying directly from her secret European city to Miami just hours after Shane returned home. Tommy went back to the case with full force. I worried that keeping Shane's activities from Tommy would do more harm than good, but Kate and Shane were adamant that we needed to stay quiet.

The situation with the cartel only escalated when Kyle's connection with Detective Ford exposed that not only was the cartel back, but their products were back on the street as well. Going on his gut assumptions and knowledge of the cartel's history, Shane met with Detective Ford and the forensics teams. With Shane's confirmation that the rims found on the burned-out SUV were the same custom rims that belonged to the cartel, the FBI had a solid link between the cartel and Rachel's death. But all they had was the connection. No other evidence was found at the scene.

There was enough evidence left that a medical examiner could do an autopsy, and he ruled that the cause of death was a suspicious overdose, not smoke inhalation. There was enough uncut heroin in her system to kill three large men. This wasn't an accident, but until more evidence was found no charges could be filed.

The death of a well-liked elementary school teacher, as well as the public's frustration with the sudden violence in the area, pushed the FBI to act quickly. Going on leads and circumstantial findings, many lower-end thugs were picked up off the streets, only to be released hours later thanks to the cartel's money-grubbing attorneys.

Fear and anxiety were my everyday companions.

My faith in Tommy's confidence that the cartel wasn't after my family lessened. My gut told me differently. Shane was hell-bent that I carry a gun, regardless of the fact that he had a handgun and that Cole and his crew were packing as well. Gun handling was not new to me; my father had insisted I learn the responsibilities of gun ownership and the proper safety protocol as soon as I could hold a pistol in my hands. But never before had I pictured using one, not until last summer, when I killed a man.

Kyle and Shane requested—no, demanded—that our family move to the family farm thirty minutes away from Mom's house. With five acres of woods and rolling hills, and with the property bordering the West River, Hollow Creek Meadows seemed to be worlds away from the hustle and bustle of the city, and it provided a safe haven for my family. It had been a thriving tobacco farm since the colonial times, and the farm had been in my mother's family for generations. After my great-grandfather passed away, my grandmother sold off all the equipment and tobacco seedlings, leaving the place to fall apart until Mom and her siblings took it over. All major work, such as the roof or furnace, were fixed immediately. All the cosmetic fixes were left for later.

Of course, Kyle, Shane, and Cole added their own enhancements to the farm when we all moved in. They installed perimeter lights, motion and vehicle detectors that surrounded the property, and a security fence and gate. We were more secure than Fort Knox. While it might have been a bit excessive, no one was taking any chances. The house may not have had central air conditioning, but it had one hell of a security plan.

"You're getting better," Shane commented after I shot the neck off an empty bottle of wine that I had finished the night before.

Shane, now fully healed a month after his latest brush with death, was my shadow for the day. If he couldn't watch over us, he would send for Cole or Cole's friend Sketch, whose appearance would frighten the most hardened criminal. Yes, I had frequently bitched about how he often he was gone, but that didn't mean I wanted him constantly up my ass. I was essentially a prisoner in my own home. He raised my paranoia with every second glance behind him or every time I saw the grim line of alertness on his lips. Our travels, when I was allowed off the property, were random and we never took the same route twice in one day. It was the paranoia that led me to take a leave of absence from Uncle Bob's office. I had enough savings, from the insurance of both the house fire and the car accident, to pay for our minimal incidentals and Katie's diapers and formula and was able to be with her at all times. There was no way I would chance leaving her at this point.

I blew a wisp of dark-brown hair out of my face,

checked the chamber and unclipped the magazine, and inhaled the aroma of hay and the sweet, warm, spring breeze. "Well I should hope so. After practicing for the last three weeks, I should at least show some improvement," I joked. I managed to hit some of the targets that were lined up near the barn. I placed the clip and safety glasses on the wooden table next to me and sat down next to Shane. "Your turn," I said, lightly smacking his denim thigh. Today had been a hard day; we'd spent most of it working on the basement in the farmhouse. After much bickering between the two of us, Mom finally suggested we take out our aggression on targets. It turned out to be a much needed distraction; we went from grump asses to smiling and talking smack the way we used to. I felt comfortable again, easy going, as if the world wasn't crumbling around us.

He stood and stretched, with his long-sleeve, navy-blue Henley shirt riding up just enough to see his toned abs. The tiny hint of flesh and ink gave me a little thrill. He took his place at the line, pulled on his gloves, and picked up his own recently acquired 9mm. (How legal and legit it was, I didn't know.) One by one, the bullets found their target. I watched Shane, his expression cold and determined, as if Christian Cruz himself were standing at the end of the range.

We took turns for an hour, with him correcting my aim and posture. By the time the handguns had been unloaded, cleaned, and put back into the cases, the breeze had picked up and a spring thunderstorm was rolling in. We were washing our hands from the manual pump inside the barn when the first drops started to fall.

"Should we chance it?" I asked, watching the fat raindrops fall harder. I handed Shane the towel.

"Nah," Shane replied as a boom of thunder shook the ground. "It's a good quarter mile back to the house. Unless you want to get soaked, we're better off here." He secured the gun cases to the back of our Kawasaki ATV. The lightning cracked close by, making me jump. Shane chuckled and stood behind me, drawing me close.

"Besides, I kinda miss having you all to myself," he whispered in my ear.

Shivers went down my spine and I closed my eyes, leaning back on his chest. It's true. We truly hadn't had a moment's peace since the fire. And now that we were living with both my mother and my aunt, every sigh and mumble was overheard. On the plus side, having an extra pair of hands around to help with Katie was very beneficial for moments like these.

"I miss this, too," I muttered. I let out a soft moan as he kissed a trail down my neck. My body clenched tightly as hot desire flooded through me. *It's been way too long.* Shane's hands roamed under my shirt and cupped my breasts. Arching into him more, the evidence of his arousal pushed against my back. I turned my head, catching his lips with mine. Fervent hunger pulsing through me, I put my hands over his as he kneaded my breasts, then trailed his hands down my stomach to the front of my jeans. Slick with need, I furiously unbuttoned my jeans and slid them down my legs, silently thankful I had thought to shave my legs that morning.

I turned around in his arms and stared into his hazel eyes now hooded in arousal. I quickly discarded my own green thermal shirt, bra, and low-rise Converses, but took my time removing Shane's clothes. Without breaking eye contact, I glided the tips of my fingers up his rib cage as I pulled his shirt over his head. I slid my fingers down and undid the button on his jeans, letting them fall to his ankles. Running my fingers over the tented bulge in his boxers, I enjoyed the hiss of breath he made as he sharply inhaled. Smiling, I take his hand and started to lightly suck each finger. Shane moaned softly as I ran his hand down the front of my body to my burning, aching core. I let out a sharp gasp as I stroked myself with his finger, in and out, fanning the flames until I couldn't take anymore. I felt myself clinch his fingers like a vice as I shattered, my mouth falling open as I leaned my head against his shoulder trembling with aftershocks.

"Baby, if I don't get inside you right now I'm going to explode," he groaned in my ear. I mewled in protest as he withdrew his hand. He grabbed his shirt from the ground and draped it across the bales of hay. Laying me down, he thrust into me, burying himself deep in one fluid motion. I moaned and threw my arms around his neck, hanging on while the wave of pleasure rose higher and higher. The thunder and rain outside our little sanctuary did little to muffle our cries as we both shattered in ecstasy.

We lay there on the stiff bales of hay, listening to each other's heartbeat and the rain hitting the roof. Shane pressed his lips to mine then stood up, pulling me up with him.

"I missed that," he muttered. I nodded. I missed that too. We had let the craziness of the cartel and parenthood, and well, life in general, push everything that was important to the side.

"Looks like the rain is stopping. We should probably head back to the house," I mentioned. I was slightly disappointed that we couldn't stay in our blissful state longer, but real life beckoned. Katie would be up from her nap by now, and while I know Mom and Aunt Nancy didn't mind watching her, I hated to take advantage of that. We threw our clothes back on and hopped on the four-wheeler. Wrapping my arms tightly around him, I pressed my cheek to his back as we took off over the dips and bumps up the hill to the main house. As we were riding along, I looked around me. I felt at home here, at peace. Regardless of what the outside world had in store for me, I would never leave here. I was home.

We made it back to the house in time to hear Katie belly laughing and the dogs barking. Smiling at Shane, I hurried through the kitchen door to find Penny and Jax running in circles and Katie in her high chair, laughing each time Penny got close.

"You don't need a sitter. Penny keeps her entertained!" Aunt Nancy said over the bells of laughter, her dark eyes dancing. My Aunt Nancy and my mom were only a year apart, but they looked identical. They even dressed similar, finding comfort in jeans and a sweatshirt. Aunt Nancy threw the broccoli she was chopping into a pot and added chunks of sharp cheddar cheese. It was my favorite dish. I snitched a chunk of cheese and inhaled the aromas of fresh rosemary bread.

"That she does," I agreed, rubbing Penny's ears. Katie reached out to me and wailed in protest when I didn't pick her up. "Aunt Nancy, I want to get cleaned up before holding her. Do you mind watching her for a few more minutes?"

"Go ahead, dear. Penny and I have it under control. But you might want to remove some of that straw from your hair. I really don't need the drains clogging up," she said, raising her eyebrows. Blushing furiously, I reached up and pulled a few golden straws just as Shane walked into the kitchen.

"Hey, baby girl, how's it—*Ow!*" he exclaimed,

rubbing the spot on his arm where I had just smacked him. "What was that for?" Glaring, I wordlessly held up the offending pieces of straw. Shane let out a snort of laughter before trying to cover it up with a cough. I rolled my eyes and grabbed his hand, pulling him up the wooden stairs to the room set aside for us.

Our bedroom was huge and could even accommodate Katie's baby gear. With sloped wood-panel ceilings, refinished dark hardwood floors, and dormer windows, it was the type of room I had wanted as a child. The en suite bathroom had been completely upgraded with a steam shower. We truly intended to hurry, keeping in mind that they were waiting on us, but one thing led to another and, well, let's just say we took a bit longer than necessary. We ambled downstairs just as Mom was putting the pot of soup on the handcrafted solid oak table.

"About time, you two. Let's eat." Aunt Nancy passed around bowls of soup and slices of her famous rosemary bread. I placed a spoon and rattle on Katie's high chair tray and took my first bite of the delicious soup. In fact, everything that my mom or Aunt Nancy made was amazing. Which is why I couldn't lose all my pregnancy weight.

"Oh Megs, your Aunt Nancy and I were thinking," Mom started, her eyes twinkling.

"It's never a good idea when you two think," I

mumbled, taking a sip of water.

"No, probably not. But that doesn't matter. We've decided this place would be the perfect home for you three."

"What?" I sputtered, choking on my water. "What are you talking about?"

"Well, I know with everything going on, you really haven't had a chance to look for houses. And Nancy mentioned something to me the other day about wanting to live full-time in Annapolis," Mom explained, passing the bread to Shane.

"Aunt Nancy, the city isn't that far away. You could get to it in a half an hour," I mentioned, confused at this sudden turn of events.

"I know. Don't get me wrong, I love it out here. But I'm tired of making the drive out and dealing with all the traffic. I'm getting too old to be doing all this manual labor," Aunt Nancy replied.

Shane and I looked at each other in silence. *Is this something we want to do?* "Aunt Nancy, that's a gracious offer. But I don't know if we have the time or the money to get involved with something like this," I said gently.

"Think about it. And it wouldn't be just you living here. The old guesthouse down the path? That would be mighty fine if someone fixed it up a bit. Just needs some paint and floorboards and it would be good as new. Your brother and Sarah could live there," Aunt Nancy continued.

"Uh, Aunt Nancy, that's something we'd have to talk to Kyle and Sarah about. Why don't we worry about that after this craziness is over," I replied, and mentally added floors, paint, an exterminator, and a new foundation to Aunt Nancy's laundry list of things to do to the guesthouse. While the thought of living on this piece of history intrigued me, the amount of work that needed to be done to the property itself, let alone the house, was mind-boggling.

After dinner, we went upstairs so Shane could check in with Kate. The tone of the conversation went from joking to serious in a matter of seconds. Shane gestured quickly for paper and a pen, all the while telling Kate to slow down.

"What's going on?" I whispered, holding the baby tighter. Shane ignored me and listened to whatever Kate was saying.

"I'll go up there tonight. Yeah, we're good. See you later." Shane clicked off the phone. "I need to go to Jersey. There's an informant that's ready to talk."

"So why are you going?"

"Because the informant said he'd only talk to me." Shane sent a text to someone, Cole I supposed.

"And don't you find that a bit suspicious?" I asked, putting fresh pajamas on Katie. Shane was busy with his phone and didn't pay attention. I picked up Katie's plush duck and threw it at his head.

"What the hell?" Shane's head shot up. "What?"

"You're not paying attention. I asked you, don't you find it the least bit suspicious that some guy you don't know is asking for you by name in Jersey? That if he's an informant, shouldn't he be talking to Kate or Rick, or hell, even Tommy?" I demanded.

"What the fuck do you want me to do? Rick and Kate vetted him, they say he's legit. They're the ones that want me to meet him," Shane shot back, throwing a sweatshirt into his backpack.

"Who is this guy? I mean, what is he to the case?" I asked wearily.

"According to Kate, he's a driver. He only has limited time, so the sooner I get up there the better."

I put Katie on my hip and followed him down the stairs. "Are you riding with Rick?"

Shane grabbed the keys to his truck. "Nope. Rick is already halfway there." He paused and kissed my lips and Katie's head. "Cole is on his way to keep an eye on you guys and should be here in thirty minutes. Kyle's also in the know and will be Cole's back up. I hate doing this, but I need to leave now. Don't go outside. Keep the Glock close."

"Yes, sir." I said with a smart-ass smirk.

Shane gave me a look. "I'm serious, Megs. Don't let anyone in except Kyle and Cole."

"Geez, what do you take me for? A fucking idiot? I know that, Shane," I raised my face up for another kiss.

"No. I don't take you for an idiot. I know you're a stubborn-ass woman." He crushed his lips to mine. "I love you anyway."

"I love you too. Be safe!" I called as he climbed into his truck. I shut the heavy door and secured the deadbolt. I walked into the space that had originally been the butler's pantry but was now a monitoring station. I ensured everything was up and running like it should be and activated the alarms. Like the tech geek he is, Kyle had managed to program all systems to send notifications to my smarter-than-me phone, so all I had to do was push a button on my phone to activate the alarms.

"Hey, Megs, want some popcorn? We're about to watch *Casablanca,*" Mom called from the kitchen. I hesitated, then declined. As much as I loved watching Humphrey Bogart, as every other woman does, being at the farm without Shane made me a bit anxious. I grabbed a bottle for Katie and climbed the stairs to our bedroom.

When my phone beeped a bit later, I admit, I jumped. Checking the screen, I smiled at Tommy's text: "Just happened to go to DQ and picked up the most awesomest peanut butter blizzard. Apparently, I'm so hot they gave me another one on the house. Do you want to share?"

Oh, hell's bells. The thought of a smooth and creamy peanut butter blizzard sounded really good, but the promise I made to Shane weighed heavy on my mind. "As awesome as that sounds, I'm good. We're going to bed. Thx anyways," I replied.

It was probably for the best anyway. I didn't need that ice cream attaching itself to my thighs. With the AC window unit humming, I curled up on the bed with Katie and flicked on the TV. I was so engrossed in a rerun of *Friends* that I didn't realize the time until Mom knocked on the door.

"Hey, babycakes, wasn't Cole supposed to be here an hour ago?" she wondered. I checked the time on my phone. *Fuck. Where was he?*

"I'm sure he got held up in traffic. There's probably an accident on Muddy Creek Road," I replied with forced confidence. "Here, take Katie and I'll text him," I said, handing her the bottle and the baby.

"Okay. Why don't you also check the monitors? That would relieve some of my worry," she said.

"Good idea." I promptly sent Cole a text, asking where the hell he was. I hurried down the stairs to check the monitors. *All the bells are on, cameras are working. So why is my stomach full of dread?* Because of our track record and the shit storm that seems to follows our family, I took the stairs two at a time and grabbed the

Glock from the case under my bed. I inserted the clip and slid the chamber back, and heard the ominous click as it loaded. Putting the safety on, I padded back down the stairs.

I checked the locks on all the windows and doors, and found nothing amiss. *Ugh, why am I so freaked out?* I put the Glock down on the kitchen table and searched for something that would distract my ever-worried mind. *Ah, chocolate pudding pie.* God help my waistline, I thought, slicing off a big hunk. The moment I sat down, the damn monitoring application on my phone beeped. Loudly. I jumped just enough at the shrill noise to bump the plate holding the chocolate pie and ended up with pie on my shirt.

"Of course the damn bad guys show up just as I'm about to eat some pie," I muttered cavalierly despite the nervous butterflies in my gut. Pushing the chair back and ignoring the large chocolate goop on my pink top, I charged over to the monitors with the Glock in hand. The activated vehicle sensor was located at the curve of River Road and since we were the only property at the dead end, there was no logical reason for anyone except Cole to venture down this way.

"Mom, why don't you take Aunt Nancy and the baby and go on downstairs," I called, gazing intensely at the screen. Not only did we have a kick-ass security system, but we also had a panic room with an emergency exit, which I was adamant about having when we moved out to the boonies. Thankfully, the old house had a root cellar with a covered and discreet exit, and fixing it up was our first priority when we moved in.

An unfamiliar vehicle passed by the first camera. Using the toggle switch, I was able to maneuver the cameras to track it. Only one car: a dark-colored SUV. I quickly noted the plate number and sent a quick text to Shane and Kyle with the info. I knew it would worry them, and I knew it could be teenagers looking for a place to hook up, but I wasn't taking any chances.

Nancy shuffled past me and went downstairs. Mom followed closely behind her, holding a sleeping Katie. The second vehicle sensor beeped. This one was hidden under the gravel that began at the driveway to the house. The vehicle was closer. I swept through the house and turned off all the interior lights, then I grabbed my gun. My heart pounded as I crouched behind the massive oak front door and gripped the heavy metal in my sweaty hands. The rule of thumb was never point your gun at something you don't want to kill. I had already killed one man, and I truly didn't want to kill again. But if someone tried to come after my family, I'd blow their ass back into the river.

CHAPTER 20

SECONDS TICKED BY like hours. Nervous sweat dripped down my back and my legs cramped. *I don't know what's worse,* I thought idly as I tried not to freak out, *the fact that someone may, in fact, try to kill us in a few seconds or that I'm not going to be able to move after staying in this position for much longer.* My cell phone, tucked into my bra, vibrated. I checked the number and saw that it was Cole.

"Where the fuck are you?" I hissed

"Coming up the drive," he replied tersely. *Coming up the drive? That didn't look like his truck.* Something wasn't right; the gut feeling I had was sending red alerts to my brain.

"You alone?"

Cole sighed. "Yeah, I'm alone. Just don't fucking shoot me when I walk through that door."

I ended the call and exhaled. Worst case scenarios and emergency plans ran through my head, and now that I knew they weren't needed I allowed myself to breathe. I flipped on the house light and sat down on the staircase in front of the door. My knees trembled and my hands shook from adrenaline. But despite his reassurance, my body froze at the sound of his footsteps on the porch.

"Megs, it's me."

I let out a shaky breath and undid the locks. "Dammit Cole, you scared me to death. I almost—" I stopped. Cole was sporting a fresh black eye and a welt across his face. "What the hell happened to you?"

He stepped inside and shut the door behind him. "I got jumped outside the gas station on Central Avenue."

"Do the other guys look worse?" I joked blandly, leading him into the kitchen. I gave him a bag of frozen peas for his face and unlocked the basement stairs. "Mom, it's clear. Cole's here."

"One guy went down, but they shot at me before I could get back up. They stole my wallet and my gun," he said grimly, sitting down at the table.

Mom and Aunt Nancy came up the stairs. They fussed and fretted over him while I took Katie upstairs. My hands shook as I changed her diaper and tucked her in.

I went back downstairs. Cole was still the center of attention and being attended to by my two favorite ladies. Chuckling at his distress, I opened up the fridge and took out two beers. Handing him one, I said, "I have a feeling you need this."

Popping the top, he took a long swig. "Yeah, I do. Thanks," he said gratefully.

I sat down across from him. "So what the hell happened?"

Cole groaned. "I was getting gas on Central Avenue when these guys come out of nowhere and hit me in the back of my head. I went down and they immediately grabbed the gun from my waistband. Then they went to town, kicking and punching me. I couldn't get up so I started kicking. I managed to kick one in the gut and that's when the asshole shot at me."

"Oh my God, you're shot?" My mom frantically looked him over. "But I don't see any blood."

"They shot *at* me. They didn't hit me," Cole snorted wearily.

"How many were there?" I asked. With Cole's size and build, there had to have been at least an army to get him down.

"At least three. The pussies got me from behind," he replied sheepishly.

"Did they say anything to you?" Aunt Nancy asked

from the stove. From the aromas coming from the pot, I could tell she was brewing some of her wicked apple elixir. The cinnamon, apple cider, and Everclear mixture was exactly what the doctor ordered.

"They didn't say anything else. The clerk inside saw it happen and he called the cops. Kyle came by. He did the walk, took my report, and wanted me to go get checked out. But then he took me aside and filled me in on what Detective Ford has been working on."

Intrigued, I leaned forward just as Mom put down a mug of the apple concoction. "What did he say? Do they have any leads?"

Cole finished his beer and went straight to the apple concoction . He took a sip of the drink and grimaced as the hot liquid went down his throat. He whistled. "Ms. Nancy, that brew of yours is strong. You'd give my old Uncle Hercle a run for his moonshine business."

"Oh hon, how do you think this family survived the wars? Tobacco was the main export, but everyone knew that this port was the place to go for what ails ya. We'd have sailors lined up at the dock down there, hoping for great-great-granny's apple elixir." Cole smiled politely and Aunt Nancy blushed. "Pardon my ramblin'. My heart can't handle all this drama. I'm going to take myself to bed." Mom agreed with her sister. Their chorus of goodnights followed them up the stairs. I waited for both bedroom doors to close before barraging Cole with more questions.

"Okay, go ahead."

Cole took another sip of the steaming liquid and set it aside. "Holy shit, Megan. I can't take any more of that. That must be, what? A hundred proof?"

"Yeah, it will hit you later if you drink much more. Aunt Nancy used to make it a lot, for parties and things like that, and more often than not, she used to have to drag my Uncle Wally to bed. It's potent stuff. But never mind the hooch, what's the latest with Detective Ford's case?"

Cole raised an eyebrow. "The VIN number for the SUV that Rachel Morrison was found in was registered to a man who died fifteen years ago, so whoever bought it used the dude's name and credit to make it look legit."

I frowned. "How does this relate to the case?"

"The former owner's grandson used to bounce at Yankee's, a strip club located on the Block, off Gay Street. After looking into the grandson, we realized that there's no way he could've gotten an SUV with his shit credit. We figured he stole his grandfather's info. But that's not what tipped our hand. Guess who owns Yankee's?" he teased.

I sighed heavily. "Christian Cruz?" I guessed.

"Close. Try Tomas Cruz, the son of Christian Cruz and the CEO of Cruz, Inc., a legit investment firm in New York City. More than likely, that investment firm is a front. The motherfucker is the face of the company, signing all the legal paperwork while Daddy does the actual deals. Because of the potential connection to the Cruz Cartel, the FBI is taking lead. Your boy, Tommy, is going to be busy for a while." Cole smirked, keeping the bag of peas on his face.

"When is he not busy? I'm just glad they finally have something to go on," I muttered, playing with the place mat.

"I have to say, having Shane take a look at the truck was pure genius on Kyle's part. We probably would have figured it out, but Shane saved everyone at least two weeks of investigation," Cole remarked, getting another beer from the fridge. Kyle, remembering what Shane had said about the cartel's custom BCBG rims, encouraged Detective Ford to talk with Shane. Thanks to Shane's history with the cartel, he was able to confirm that the rims on the burned-out SUV were, in fact, the same rims that were at the safe house after the explosion, and the same custom rims that the cartel required their upper-level management to have on their vehicles.

Huh. I guess Shane's involvement isn't just a pain in my ass. "So what happened to your truck?" I asked, remembering the monitor.

"The clowns who jumped me punctured three of my tires. Sketch came and I grabbed his truck while he waited for the tow. I took a roundabout route to get here to make sure no one was following me." Cole stood and poured the rest of Aunt Nancy's apple pie cider into the sink. "That stuff is dangerous."

"What now?" I inquired. "How much longer are we going to have to sit on pins and needles?"

Cole shrugged. "Well, that depends on what happens with Shane, Rick, and the informant. From what Rick tells me, this dude is legit and is more than willing to squeal for the right price."

A thought occurred to me. "Is Tommy in the know? I mean, does he know about your and Shane's involvement?"

Cole closed his eyes and thought for a minute. "Not everything. For instance, he doesn't know about Shane's involvement. When I spoke with Kate earlier today, she was hell-bent on keeping as much info away from Tommy as she could."

I smacked the table in frustration. "Why? What the hell is the purpose of keeping this from him? Especially now that the FBI has reinvested their energy into the cartel case?"

Cole scowled. "Kate is going with her instincts. She doesn't trust Tommy."

"Why not? Is there something you all aren't telling me?"

Cole heaved a heavy sigh. "Kate has been looking at all the angles down in Miami. She traced a few of the mid-level cartel guys to a boat slip in a Miami Beach marina. She noticed that the marina was owned by CTG Holding Company. The same marina where a large forty-foot yacht was docked."

I shrugged. "Okay. What does that have to do with Tommy?"

Cole rubbed his beard. "Most of Tommy's investments are in some way affiliated with CTG Holdings. His grandfather was on the board of directors of CTG Holdings."

I shook my head. "They have a lot of money and investments; I'm not surprised that they have a marina," I retorted, confused at where this conversation was going.

"Yeah, but the funny thing is, the suspect she was tracking had no trouble walking around as if he owned the yachts. Now, this isn't conclusive. Who knows what kind of background check they do on slip rentals. So it could be all one big coincidence. But…" his voice trailed off.

"But you don't believe in coincidences," I finished, my voice faltering. "Do you really think Tommy's grandfather was with the cartel?"

"Not sure, but it's one more piece of the puzzle. An ever expanding puzzle."

I groaned and buried my face in my hands. "Unless we get a witness and a smoking gun, we're going be running from the cartel for the rest of our lives."

"God, I hope not. Life wouldn't be worth living if you're constantly in fear," Cole surmised.

I stood up and stretched. "I'm going to bed. Are you going to be up for a while?"

"Darlin', I'm not here to sleep. When Kyle or Shane comes back, I'll head out to the guest house."

I smiled. "Well, thanks for coming over. Good night."

Cole smiled and tipped the brim of his baseball cap. "Good night, Megs."

I left Cole in the kitchen and ambled up the stairs. The moon, full and bright, was glistening off the West River. The steady buzz of the cicadas and the whirl of the air conditioning unit provided the soundtrack for the night. I checked on Katie, who was sleeping on her tummy with her little bum in the air, blissfully unaware of how dangerous our lives were. *If only it were that easy, to sleep the fear away.*

I climbed into bed and sent Shane a goodnight message. I didn't expect a text back; he was probably just arriving in New Jersey to meet with Rick. I tossed and turned; my body was exhausted but my mind wouldn't stop reeling. *Living like this is going to push me to the brink of insanity.* I would love to get away from all this madness, at least until the bastards were caught. The wheels in my head turned until I finally fell asleep and dreamed of seagulls and warm sandy beaches.

***

I woke six hours later to Katie talking to herself in her crib. I had left the shutters open so the room was full of light from the rising sun. Rubbing the sleep out of my eyes, I shuffled over to Katie and changed her diaper, and the two of us headed downstairs.

"Morning," I mumbled to Cole as I passed by the butler's pantry. He was so engrossed in his laptop that he didn't even look up. "See Katie, men are addicted to technology the way women are obsessed with handbags, shoes, and smutty books," I whispered in her ear. I grabbed a bottle from the fridge and took her back into the family room. While Katie ate her breakfast, I flipped on the TV to watch the news.

"Cole, come here and look at this," I called. The anchor mentioned the cartel case and that an update was just coming in.

"Yeah, I just read a note from Kate. This isn't good," Cole cursed, walking into the room.

"What do you mean?" I asked, but before Cole could respond, the blonde anchor spoke.

"The Cruz Cartel is notorious in cities such as Philadelphia, Trenton, Camden, and Miami. However, new reports show that the Cruz Cartel is now operating in Baltimore and the surrounding suburbs." The camera cut to a press conference being held in front of the

Maryland State Police station in Glen Burnie. Detective Ford appeared at the podium.

"We have reason to believe that the death of twenty-eight-year-old Rachel Marie Morrison and the double homicide at the Double J's in Edgewater, which took the lives of Haley Dale and undercover officer, Mark Sinclair, are connected. The clues that we have found point to the Cruz Cartel. We are asking for the public's help in solving these terrible crimes. Please come forward if you have any statements or facts related to these cases. We have a tip line set up and your call will remain anonymous. At this time, I'd like to introduce the agency representative we're working with, Mr. Thomas Greene from the Federal Bureau of Investigations." Detective Ford stepped back to give Tommy room at the podium. My eyes zeroed in on Tommy, taking in the crisp gray suit and navy-blue button-down shirt. His short blond hair was perfectly trimmed and his green eyes sharp as ever. His presence was official, almost political looking.

"Good morning. I'd like to thank the Maryland State Police and the local districts of Crofton, Edgewater, and Baltimore City for their help in connecting these cases. Now I want to urge all of you out there to think about what is taking place. These people are hurting our families, our neighborhoods, and even our livelihoods. If you know anything about these cases or have information that could lead to an arrest, please call the number below. Thank you for your help." I sat back on the couch and turned to Cole, who looked like he wanted to punch the television.

"Explain to me how this is bad?" I asked Cole, as Mom came down the stairs. "Good morning," I said to her. Not awake until at least two cups of coffee are in her system, my greeting was acknowledged with a flick of the wrist as she went into the kitchen.

"According to Kate and Rick, Tommy now knows everything. Thanks to an IT glitch, he was granted access to a database that Kate set up. She had to bring him up to speed. He knows that we've connected his father, or his father's company, to the boat slip in Miami. He knows that we've connected the cartel to the club in Baltimore, and he knows about the confirmation of rims in Rachel's homicide. Because of all that, Tommy is now fully aware of Kyle and Shane's involvement."

"Look, I know you believe that Tommy would protect his father first but you've got that all wrong. Tommy has never put anything before his allegiance to his country. The mission, the job, the case—those are what are number one in his mind. He missed his younger sister's high school graduation because he had to take a field test for the FBI. He would miss his own wedding if he was involved in a case."

Despite our past, I felt the need to defend Tommy. He lived and breathed the cases he worked on. When we were engaged, I didn't see him for days at a time because he was that diligent and loyal to his work. Tommy never left a stone unturned, and I couldn't imagine the betrayal he must have felt when his former partner told him that his own father, a stuck-up investment banker, had dealings with the Cruz Cartel.

"You're probably right. But Kate had her reasons. She wouldn't get Shane involved if she ultimately didn't have to. And if she felt she could trust Tommy, she would have given him the information long ago. Don't forget that Kate and Rick never found the mole that leaked your location to the cartel, so who the hell knows what's going to happen when they get wind of Shane's confirmation of the rims, let alone his meeting with that informant in New Jersey."

My stomach dropped. *Fuck. This is never going to end.* "You don't think anyone is going to come forward?"

Cole rubbed the day-old stubble on his cheek. "I didn't say that. The tide could turn in one of three ways: pushers get turned in and the public outcry forces the cartel out of Maryland, or they scatter in the wind like they did the last time, making it more difficult to put any more pieces together. Or they lay low for now and go after everyone and anyone who could name them in a case. Either justice or greed will prevail. We won't know what will happen until it happens."

Great. I thought about everything Cole said for a

minute. Then Katie squawked, needing to be burped. I patted her back and looked out of the expansive picture window overlooking the river. Everything was serene and quiet. *How long will it take for our lives to go back to normal?*

Cole received a text. He read it and grinned. "Your man is five minutes away. Hopefully he has some good news for us."

"He better," I replied dryly. I stood and placed Katie in her portable swing, then headed into the kitchen for some much needed caffeine. Mom was sitting at the table, nursing her mug.

"I'm somewhat coherent now. Did I hear you all mention something about justice or greed prevailing? Or was I still half asleep?" she asked tiredly.

Cole and I gave her the ten-cent version of what happened. My mother never asked for specifics, and only ever wanted to be told what she needed to know. She respected the danger that Shane, Cole, and Kyle were putting themselves in and hearing less allowed her a little bit more sleep at night. We had just finished up when the sensor alerted us that Shane's truck was pulling into the driveway. With a smile, I picked up Katie and stood in the doorway just as he was driving up to the house.

Weary and bone-tired, Shane slowly dragged himself into the house. With dark stubble dotting his face and wearing the same clothes he'd left in, he looked like he'd gone through the hell.

"Hey, baby. Are you okay?"

Shane nodded. "I'm just beat. I drove all night to get here."

Cole came out of the kitchen and gave Shane one of those one-armed man hugs. "Shane. How's Jersey?"

Shane chortled and rolled his eyes. "A fucking mess, as always. Are they always doing highway construction?"

Ignoring their banter, I asked the question everyone was dying to know. "Did you talk to the informant? What did he say?"

Shane sat down on the stairs and shucked off his work boots. "Yeah, I spoke with him. I hadn't met him before, but he heard about me through his dealings with the upper level guys. That's why he asked for me by name. Rick promised him witness protection and he sang like a bird. He had trip logs, phone numbers and hierarchies, firsthand accounts of drug transactions. He'll tell us whatever we want to know."

Jubilation coursed through me as I let out a yell of relief. "Are you fucking kidding me? It's over?"

Shane's face turned grave. "It's not even close to being over. This guy—his name is Henrico Philips—he has names and dates and that's about it, and anything he gives to us isn't hard evidence. But this is the big break that the FBI needs. Once they start connecting the dots, that's when people will start going away. And you better believe the cartel is going to be after this guy."

I forced the memory of last summer to the back of my mind. I remembered what it was like, having someone find out where you were. During my period in protective custody, someone, somehow, had found out our location and we barely escaped with our lives. "He will have protection, right?"

Shane nodded. "He'll be deep in protection; only a few people will know where he is."

"Well, we know how well that went last time," Mom pointed out, refilling her mug from the carafe.

Shane winced. "You're right about that. From what Kate tells me, the whole incident last summer turned the entire witness protection section around. Security is tighter and there are fewer people in the know."

"What do we do now? Wait?" Nancy asked, taking the orange juice out of the fridge.

"We wait and stay vigilant. At this point, we have no idea what, or even if, anything will come out of this new update. We don't want to become lax and be taken off guard," Cole stated, crossing his thick arms.

"So we wait," Mom said firmly. *And so we wait. And go completely insane with cabin fever while we do so.*

CHAPTER 21

ONE BY ONE, THE CARTEL'S soldiers came falling down. A week after the FBI's cry for the public's help, numerous calls came into the Baltimore field office with tips about the cartel. Some were as phony as a three-dollar bill, but some actually panned out. These were calls from concerned citizens, tired of the cartel and the gangs wreaking havoc in their neighborhoods. Community groups banded together to push out the drugs and the gunfights, and they were making progress. Despite Cole's insistence that we needed to stay vigilant and stay on guard, the information coming from Tommy and Kate pointed to the opposite. Tommy was furious at Shane and Cole's involvement, but there wasn't anything he could do. According to them, the cartel leadership had lawyered up and most of the minions were either in jail, dead, or had somehow vanished. Of course, Henrico, the driver, had not yet testified, but the information he was providing to the FBI had been fruitful.

Unfortunately, the murder of Rachel Morrison was still unsolved. But the FBI, in conjunction with the Maryland State Police and the DEA, had pieced together some leads. Tommy was at the forefront of this crusade and I had never been more proud of him. Even Shane had to begrudgingly commend him on the actions he'd taken so far.

Despite all the seemingly good news and progress that was being made, as the days grew longer and the temperature rose, my patience dwindled. Shane and I fought over everything: the lack of sex, his refusal to get up with Katie, him not allowing me to leave the house. The walls of the old house felt like they were closing in on me. I needed to escape. More than that, I needed to breathe.

"Argh, I need a break!" I grumbled, rubbing the sleep from my eyes. Katie's wails grated my poor sleep-deprived mind. Taking the pillow from underneath my head, I unceremoniously whacked Shane on his stomach with it. At nine in the morning, his ass was still in bed. Never mind the fact that Katie had me up four times during the night and was fully awake by five thirty.

He didn't hear her cry, yet he heard the text message alert and was wide awake. I had just put her down forty minutes ago for a much-needed nap.

"Wake up," I ordered. Shane rolled onto his stomach with a snort. "Shane, I'm not kidding."

"I got her earlier," came his mumbled reply.

"For real? We're keeping track now? You really don't want to go there with me," I snapped as I got out of bed. I walked over to her white crib. Katie reached her chubby arms out for me and my heart ached at the sight of her tears. I carried her over to the changing table and undid her pajamas.

"Why don't we go to the beach? Get away from here for a few days," I offered, partially as a peace offering but mostly to keep him awake.

"Are you serious?" Shane asked, his voice muffled by the pillows.

"Yeah, why the hell not?" I bristled, putting Katie into her third set of pajamas.

For the last two days, my poor baby had been having massive explosions in her diaper and her bum was redder than a lobster. I checked her temperature with the ear thermometer. Yep, and a low-grade fever to boot. She screamed when I put a layer of diaper cream on her and my anxiety rose a bit more. I hated hearing her cries of pain. "Oh, baby girl, I know it hurts."

After putting her down into her crib and cringing

at her shrill cries, I dressed quickly, then picked up my tear-stained five-month-old and held her close. As I walked out of the room, I called over my shoulder to Shane, "Get dressed. We're taking her to the doctor in five minutes." I didn't give him the chance to respond. Frankly, I didn't care if he went with me or not; we needed time out of the house away from each other.

I had Katie strapped into her car seat by the time Shane thundered down the stairs. He had thrown on some baggie cargo pants and a blue, short-sleeve, button-down shirt; he left it untucked to cover the bulge of the handgun in his waistband.

"Really? You're bringing a handgun to the pediatrician's office?" I shot at him, picking up the heavy carrier and walking out to my SUV. Shane ignored me and climbed into the driver's seat. He removed the Glock from his pants and put it under the seat. We drove the twenty minutes to Dr. Andrew's office in Edgewater in strained silence. In fact, we didn't speak to each other during the visit either. If Dr. Andrew noticed the tension, he didn't mention it.

With a diagnosis of a virus and prescriptions for an ointment and a probiotic in hand, I had just secured the car seat and gotten into the car when Shane turned to face me. I steeled myself for a confrontation.

"I'm going to say this for the last time and then I'm done talking about it. You and Katie are my life; I will not lose you to the cartel. Yes, I know it's frustrating to have to stay at the farm. Yes, I know how much you want to go back to work and how much you want your old life back. But your old life is gone. You need to quit your damn whining and let me do what I need to do to protect you," he said quietly, almost ominously.

"I made one fucking comment, Shane. One suggestion about going on vacation, like normal people do. I don't take for granted what you or Kyle or Cole have done for this family, but there is a light at the end of the tunnel and, dammit, I'm not ashamed to be looking forward to a time when I'm not running in fear. I have not once whined about staying at the farm, but I have made my opinion quite clear on what you do when you're not at home. I hate that you go out looking for trouble, that you go out cruising the streets with your boys in search of someone that will get you killed," I shot back, fury fueling my words.

"I'm doing what I have to do to keep this family safe!" Shane bellowed, causing me to jump. A millisecond later, Katie's cries permeated the vehicle. "Fuck!" Shane growled.

"Really, Shane? Jesus Christ, can you be any more of an asshole?" I jumped out of the car, flung the back door open, and reached in to unhitch the car seat. I placed the seat gently on the sidewalk, then I walked over to the driver side window. "Just fucking go. You obviously need a time-out and I don't want deal with your bullshit right now. I'll call Kyle for a ride."

"Fine," Shane replied with a hiss. His anger darkened his hazel eyes. He threw my SUV into drive and peeled out of the parking lot and onto Mayo Road.

Tears prickled behind my eyes as I rooted through the diaper bag for my phone. Luckily, Kyle's precinct was right down the road.

"Hey Kyle, can you do me a huge favor?" I asked my baby brother when he answered the phone.

Five minutes later, I had Katie safely secured into the squad car and we were driving back down Muddy Creek Road. Kyle was furious that Shane would leave me at the doctor's office unprotected.

"Come on, Kyle. It's not like the cartel is able to follow every movement I make. Like they'd really be staking out the pediatrician's office on the off chance that Katie would get diaper rash and diarrhea."

"I know, but for someone who is hell-bent on making sure you're safe, he looks like the biggest dumbass for just leaving you behind." Kyle's stared at the road.

"I know. We're all getting a bit antsy. We've been at each other's throats lately," I whispered sadly. I knew that we just needed to get past this whole cartel business. But at what cost? I felt our relationship spiraling downward.

We pulled into the long driveway. Mom and Aunt

Nancy were sitting on the front porch waiting for us, thanks to my quick text message explaining what had happened. Cole's beat-up truck sat off to the side.

"Where's Shane?" Mom asked.

"He didn't come back?" Worried thoughts swirled around my head, but I pushed them aside. *He's probably letting off some steam.*

"Nope. Cole just came by, said that he has a new message from Kate," Mom replied. I unloaded Katie from the car and Mom took the car seat out of my hands and took her inside. Kyle and I followed her into the house, the solid oak floors echoing our footsteps. Kyle went straight for the massive kitchen in the back while Mom, Aunt Nancy, and I headed into the family room.

"What did Dr. Andrew say?" Mom asked, pulling a sleeping Katie out of her seat.

I fell into the oversized couch and curled my feet underneath me. "He said it's just a virus. He gave me a prescription for an ointment and a probiotic and said for us to give her Tylenol for the fever. He also said we can start her on solids now. Bananas will help."

"That makes sense." She laid Katie on the couch and changed her diaper like a pro, adding some of the soothing ointment. Katie didn't even blink; she was so tired. "Now, what happened with Shane?"

I explained what was said earlier and the issues we were having. The house wasn't huge, so I knew she overheard our arguments. She agreed that any relationship under this amount of stress would fracture.

"You two need some time away to sort everything out. To be a couple. You've had this death threat over your heads for your entire relationship. No wonder you're at odds with each other," Mom said gently.

Aunt Nancy agreed. "Why don't you two go away for the upcoming weekend? Just go to the beach for some fun in the sun; you don't have to go far. Uncle Bob has a house in Ocean City. Why don't you talk to him about using that?"

Their suggestions sounded great, but I didn't want to leave Katie behind. And did I really want to be with Shane for three days by myself? I mean, yeah, it would be great to spend time with him, but would we fight the entire time?

"I don't know, Mom. I don't know if I want to leave Katie while she's sick. And I don't want to leave you unprotected," I ventured. But Mom pish-poshed my concern.

"Katie will be fine. But if you're worried, we'll have Kyle and Sarah stay here with us."

Kyle walked into the family room carrying a plate piled high with sandwiches and chips. "Why are we staying here?"

Mom raised her eyebrows at the plate. "Please tell me you didn't use the last of the ham. I was planning to make ham and bean soup with that."

Kyle smiled sheepishly. "I only used a small bit. The rest is turkey and chicken. But don't sidetrack me. Please tell me why my wife and I are moving in?"

Aunt Nancy spoke up, "Megan and Shane need some time away. If Kate and Cole think we need someone armed in the house, then you can come stay with us."

Mom waved her hand at the notion. "Armed person, my ass. I know my way around a firearm. But if it would make you feel better, we'd love to have you both here. I haven't spent much time with you two lately. It would be nice to catch up."

The look of dread on Kyle's face had me in stitches. "You know, a few days at the beach sounds great. I think Cole would be fine here. You know the man can't cook worth a darn and it would give you an excuse to drive someone else...er...I mean, care for someone new," Kyle interjected.

Mom gave him a knowing look. "I don't care who goes or stays, we just need to make sure all our bases are covered. Nancy and I can take care of Katie," she stood up with my now-awake baby and stalked off toward the kitchen.

"You're such a wimp," I whispered to Kyle.

"Oh, please. What did I tell you last time? I like my marital benefits. We're still in the honeymoon phase, meaning we still hump like rabbits. Do you honestly think I could get it up with Mom in the next room?"

I burst out laughing. "Oh, Lordy. I don't want to know!"

"But for real, if we need to cool our jets for three days I'm sure we could. But before you all go traipsing off into the sunset, let's double-check with Tommy and Kate to get their take on the situation. With all these arrests lately, this may be the prime time to get away."

***

SHANE DIDN'T COME home until after dinner. With barely a wave, he wordlessly walked straight up to the bedroom.

"Oh, boy. Wish me luck," I muttered to Mom. Picking up Katie to serve as my shield, I walked upstairs and found him sitting on the bed.

"Hey," I said softly. I made myself appear busy by changing the baby's diaper.

"Hey."

Yeah, this is going to be a struggle. "Are we going to talk about what happened?" I asked gently, sitting next to him and putting Katie on the bed between us.

"What's there to talk about? I can't do anything about it. We're constantly at each other's throats. I'm not happy here; neither are you. What more can we do aside from sit on our collective asses and wait for the whole thing to die down?" he retorted, running his hand through his short hair.

"I don't know, but we have to do something before this situation reaches the point of no return. We can't just stay like this...not for much longer."

"I know."

I traced my finger along the rough skin of his knuckles. I loved that he worked with his hands. Calloused and firm, his hands fixed machines and created magic in the bedroom. I missed that magic. "No other relationship could endure what ours has. We have to be strong. But we both have to try. If it's only one of us, then there ends up being resentment," I whispered.

"Yeah."

Seriously, what the fuck is with all these simple answers? I wanted to scream, to shout, to do something to get his attention and get him to show *something,* some emotion other than brooding.

"We need to get back to being Shane and Megan, the couple. Maybe if we go away for the weekend, we can get things back on track."

Shane didn't respond so I gripped his hand. "Shane, I need to know what you're thinking. Please talk to me," I begged.

"It's not that I don't love you. I do. God, I do. But I have this feeling in my stomach that we're fighting a losing battle. That everything we've tried to protect and to save will be for nothing in the end," he said somberly.

A hysterical sob rose up in my throat as I grabbed his shoulders and pulled him into me, pressing Katie between us. "Don't think that. Please don't think that. We're tough, you and me. We're going to get through this. There's no if, ands, or buts about it. We've hit a rough patch, that's it. We'll get through this bullshit," I swore through my tears, but he was stoic. "Shane, dammit, listen to me. You told me you trekked across the country to find me. You risked your life for me. We have a kid together. You better believe I'm in it for the long haul. Don't fucking think that we're not going to be anything other than fine."

Tears shone in Shane's eyes and he looked at me sadly. "I'm scared out of my mind that I can't protect you. A day doesn't go by when I don't see a vision of you dead. That our entire family is—dead. And it's all my fault." My heart dropped. The finality of his tone worried me more than his words. It was as if our demise were a foregone conclusion. He exhaled a broken gasp. "Baby, the cartel tortured women in front of me. They raped women right in front of me to get me to crack. They would call those women by your name to fuck with my head. And, baby, they did. My mind is a hundred ways fucked up. I can't stop seeing those women in my dreams. Hearing their screams, their pleas for help. God, it echoes in my head constantly. I can't get rid of it."

My mouth gaped as I fought back the tears. The

terror those women endured, all because the cartel wanted to torture the man who held my heart. I pushed the nauseating thought away. "Why didn't you tell me?"

"Because the moment I saw you, I saw the life in your eyes. I didn't want to scare you or make the situation between us even worse. You were alive, and that's all that mattered."

I leaned forward so our foreheads touched. "I don't know what to say."

Shane gave a shaky chuckle. "I don't know what to say, either."

I kissed him gently on the lips. "I shouldn't have brought up the vacation. With Katie and everything going on, I think I just met my limit."

Shane nodded. "You and me both, baby. But maybe you're right. Maybe a weekend away would do us a world of good."

I wiped away my tears and gave him a small smile. "So, we're going to try? You're with me on this?"

"I'm with you, babe. All the way." The smile he returned was tentative, but it didn't reach his eyes. The lead weight of dread sat heavy on my heart, and I wondered what we were in for.

CHAPTER 22

THE NEXT DAY I CALLED Uncle Bob to see if we could use his beach house for the weekend. Thankfully, he was fine with it. This started a flurry of activity. First, we called Kate, who was surprised at our request. She surmised that Tommy would be the best person to talk to since he was in charge, so we called him. After playing phone tag, he finally conceded that it would be all right to leave—as long as everyone went. He didn't have the manpower to send anyone to Ocean City to provide protection for us except for Rick. With Kyle working the case alongside Detective Ford and the force already stretched to its limits, we would have been leaving my family to chance.

So the romantic weekend away turned into a family

vacation. Not exactly what I had wanted, but whatever. We were going away; that's all that mattered. The very thought of planning for the weekend was such a mood booster that for the rest of the week Shane and I actually smiled more at each other and acted more like we had in the past.

Finally, the weekend came.

As we sped down Route 50 and over the Chesapeake Bay Bridge with the windows open, the stress began to lift. We stayed on Route 50, cruising down through the rural roads of Maryland's Eastern Shore. When the bridge that crosses the Isle of Wright Bay came into view, a tingle of excitement washed over me and I shrieked with happiness. Of course, Shane looked over at me as if I was a dumb ass, but I didn't care!

As we made our way along, turning left onto North Philadelphia Street, nostalgia hit me. The perfume of ocean air mixed with the smell of suntan lotion and a tinge of sweetness from Dolly's Candy Shoppe was the perfect welcome back to my home away from home. We used to spend a week at Uncle Bob's every summer when I was growing up. Nothing had changed. The sidewalks were still crowded with families, the seagulls were rabid for a bite to eat, and the traffic sucked. We drove five miles down to 81st Street and Coastal Highway where my uncle's three-story townhouse was located, right on the beach.

I was out of the car before Shane could put it in park. Stretching, I inhaled the salty air. "Oh, how I've missed this place. Can I just tell you again how freaking excited I am to be here?"

Shane got out and looked around. "Now that we're here, I'm pretty psyched too. It's been a while since I've been here. This town hasn't changed a bit."

He grabbed our suitcase and portable crib while I took Katie inside. Seeing the view of the Atlantic Ocean from the balcony made me giddy with anticipation.

Claiming the largest room in the house, Shane dropped the portable crib and suitcase onto the navy-blue comforter. Laughter trickled in from the lower level announcing the arrival of Mom and Nancy, followed by Cole and Rick.

"Do not *ever* make us drive with your mom *ever* again," Cole grumbled, bringing in a crate full of electronic equipment.

I picked Katie up out of her car seat and wiped the drool from her chin. "Oh, what's wrong Cole? Did she try to fix you up with someone? Help you work out your love life?"

Rick snorted as he headed to the bedroom across the hall. "Try to fix him up? She practically married him off to your cousin Heather. I think she had the guest list already set."

I choked on my laughter and ended up snorting. We

quickly got settled in. Mom and Aunt Nancy went out for groceries while Shane and I took Katie for a walk on the beach.

"As much as I like Cole, and even Rick, I really can't wait until we have some privacy," I said, glancing over my shoulder at our two "bodyguards" who were standing on the balcony watching us with binoculars. For a Friday afternoon, the beach was virtually empty, except for the seagulls scavenging for picnic remnants.

"I hear ya," Shane muttered. He was busily texting God knows who.

"It's a beautiful day, Shane. We're at the beach. What's so important you can't look up from your phone?" I asked as I adjusted Katie in her wrap against me.

"It's not important. Just working something out." He slid his phone into his back pocket. I reached for his hand just as his phone vibrated.

"Shoot. Hang on. Let me get that." He turned and walked toward the water out of my earshot.

Is he serious? What is so private that he can't have a conversation in front of me? I watched him talk animatedly on the phone. Listening to Katie's babble did little to divert my attention from him pacing across the sand. The furrowed brow, clenched jaw, rapid hand gestures—yep, he was pissed. *Sure glad I'm not on the other end of that call,* I thought with a smirk. Five minutes later, Shane walked back to us.

"What's that all about?" I asked as he stalked toward the house.

"Nothing," came his grumble.

Here we go again.

"What the hell happened, Shane? Who was that on the phone?" I demanded, huffing and puffing from the exertion of trying to run through sand with a twenty-pound baby strapped to my chest.

"Just a misunderstanding, that's all. I'm starved. Let's see if Mom wants crabs for dinner." He gave a big, albeit, fake smile. His let's-pretend-everything's-okay smile. Whatever.

"What aren't you telling me?" I continued. Part of me wanted to stay at the beach and try to talk it through. The other part, the trying-not-to-be-a-drama-queen part, just wanted to let it go.

"Babe, it's nothing. This douche was getting under my skin about something at work. I did something for him a while back and now he's pissed because I won't do it again," Shane said. We reached the house and he turned on the hose to wash the sand off our feet and then followed me inside.

"We got some stuff for breakfast and lunch, but figured we could get crabs tonight," Mom said as we walked up the stairs. She reached for her granddaughter, whom I gratefully handed over. I arched my back to stretch.

"Crabs sound great. I'll head up to the shack on 130th Street. They always have the best deals," Shane mentioned, his eyes back on his phone.

"Mom, would you mind watching her?" I pulled my purse off the hook, but Shane grabbed my hand.

"Nah, babe, you stay. Take a nap. Me and Cole got this," he said with a smile. I arched my eyebrows at his excitement, then shrugged. I didn't want to deal with his roller coaster moods.

"Get some shrimp and beer too."

"Gotcha." With a quick peck on the lips, he thundered down the stairs with Cole.

What just happened? Did I miss something? *Why is he so excited to get crabs?* Suspicion weighed heavily in my stomach and I didn't know what to think. But one thing I did know was that I was tired of always being suspicious. Just tired.

***

"Hey, babe, you ready to eat?"

"Hmmm?" I opened my eyes, momentarily confused as to why I was sleeping on the balcony. Then I remembered coming out to read on the chaise lounge and nodding off during a very hot and steamy scene between a wealthy billionaire and his innocent, yet oh-so-sexy, lover.

"The smut must not have been that good," Shane smirked, helping me up.

"Nope, not as good as the real thing," I replied dryly. He smirked and slung his arm over my shoulders.

"Nothing is ever as good as the real thing."

True, but when smut is the only thing you've gotten recently... I pushed away the bitterness and flashed him a big smile. "Of course not."

Everyone filtered through the sliding glass doors, their arms laden with the supplies necessary to eat crabs. Rick spread out the stacks of newspapers onto the table. Cole was right behind him with paper bags full of fresh steamed Maryland blue crabs and steamed shrimp, all coated with Maryland's own Old Bay Seasoning. Mom brought the paper towels, mallets, and crackers, and Aunt Nancy brought out the melted butter. Shane passed out the beers and I buckled Katie into her portable swing. Soon we tucked into a true Maryland feast. Picking crabs was a rite of passage, with most kids in Maryland learning how to pick their first blue at an early age. As I gently pulled the succulent meat from the crab claw, I closed my eyes in delight and reveled in the taste. After stuffing ourselves silly for over two hours, we cleaned up the mess and washed the spicy seasoning off our lips and hands.

"Why don't you guys go down to the boardwalk?

I'm too stuffed to move. Leave Katie with me. You guys go have fun," Mom said with a smile. She was already situated in front of the TV with her crochet yarn in her lap.

"What do you think, Katie Lou? Do you wanna stay with Grandma?" I asked a sleepy Katie who was sitting in Aunt Nancy's lap. Mom had already bathed her and put her in her pajamas while we were cleaning up the crab shells. Katie's beautiful brown eyes drifted closed while she drank her milk.

"What do you think, babe? Wanna head down to good ole Playland? I bet I can beat you at some Skee-ball," I teased, looking at Shane, who was engrossed in his phone furiously texting. "Shane!"

"What? Oh, sorry, Megs. Yeah, let's head on down there," he replied absentmindedly. Of course, he had escaped cleanup duty and was freshly showered. I rolled my eyes and went to the bedroom to put Katie in her bed, then jumped into the shower to wash the smell of crab off my skin.

Thirty minutes later, I walked back into a practically empty living room.

"Where did the guys go?" I asked Mom.

"They're out on the balcony," she replied, her crochet needle working furiously.

I moved toward the balcony, but low arguing voices stopped me in my tracks. *What the hell is going on?* Shane leaned against the railing with his arms crossed and a scowl on his face while Cole chewed him out.

"What the hell is going on?" I demanded, sliding the door open. Cole stopped midsentence and threw his hands in the air.

"Nothing, just old bullshit," Shane moved passed me and slapped his faded red cap on his head. "Ready?"

"Yeah. Are you coming, Cole?"

"Yep. Rick's staying here with your mom. I think she promised him apple turnovers."

After saying good-bye, the three of us trooped downstairs, climbed into the SUV, and made our way down Coastal Highway to the inlet, where the infamous boardwalk awaited us. With two amusement parks, games, and all the junk food you could think of, it was my favorite place in the world. It took forever to find a place to park—the summertime crowds were larger than I remembered from previous years—and as we walked toward the boardwalk, we were bumped and jostled every which way.

We reached the boardwalk and I inhaled the tantalizing aromas of funnel cake, caramel corn, and taffy. I grabbed Shane's hand and pulled him into the line for the fried yumminess.

"Have I told you how much I love you?" I asked with a big smile, wrapping my arms around him.

His hazel eyes danced as he caught my stare. "Not

recently, no."

"Well, I love you so much. And I'm low on cash, so you get to buy me a funnel cake," I teased, tucking my hands into his back pockets. My hand grazed something small and plastic. "What's this?" I pulled back, taking the object with me. To my horror, I held a small plastic bag filled with white powder.

Please tell me this isn't what I think it is. I had taken a mandatory drug and alcohol class in high school, so I was well versed on what the white powder substance could be. *What the hell? Why does he have coke in his pocket? Is he using? Dealing?* Hundreds of scenarios ran through my head.

"What is this?" I asked in a low voice. Shane cursed and pulled me out of the line and into the shadows outside the arcade.

"Baby, I…" he struggled for the words, the excuses.

"*Baby* nothing! What the fuck are you doing with coke?" My body tensed, ready for a fight. Of all the harebrained shit he'd pulled throughout the year, having coke on him was the worst.

"It's not mine," he said in a rush, "I'm meeting this girl…"

"You're meeting a girl? What the fuck? Why?"

"Will you let me finish? It's for the case. We set up a buy to go down this weekend. This chick I was going to meet was willing to travel here for the deal. That's why

I was on the phone earlier."

For the case my ass. "You're making a drug deal on *our* vacation? Are you kidding me, right now? Why the hell would you even consider doing something like that?" I seethed, balling my fists. The urge to deck him for his stupidity was overwhelming; it took everything I had to maintain some control.

"Why the hell do you think Tommy and the crew were so easily convinced that we should come here? We think this chick is dating Christian Cruz's son. If I can get to her, finesse her a bit, get something going, she'll lead us right to him. Tommy said that the only way we could come here was if I agreed to the buy. But something came up; the chick I was supposed to meet is still in Baltimore, so the buy was canceled." He towered over me. No matter. The anger running through my veins made me feel ten feet tall.

"So that's the real reason you wanted to come up here? You didn't want to get away with me? To try to get back what we've lost? No. It was all for the case." The bitter taste in my mouth was making me nauseous as I tried to keep the tears from falling.

"I didn't say that," he said carefully as he reached for my hand. I yanked it back; I knew once he touched me, my resolve would crumble.

"Don't touch me. You're not allowed to touch me. Start from the damn beginning. I want the truth." I stepped away from him and crossed my arms.

"Tommy has an undercover drug task force called The Syndicate. Mostly former DEA agents, gangbangers, and FBI – these guys know their drugs and how to push product. Their covers have never been blown, so they have credibility. The chick I was meeting is supposedly dating the son of Christian Cruz. And apparently the cartel is looking for a new supplier. They've been hyping up The Syndicate so much that the cartel asked for a buy," he said, running his hands through his short hair.

"Why would they come to Ocean City, of all places, for a buy with a supplier?" I asked, my voice tight with tension.

"We think they're moving everything by boat, and with the marinas and international waters only twelve miles out, it's an easier escape route than the port of Baltimore. But we don't know much more than that. The son is an enigma. We haven't been able to find him—he's a ghost. He seems only to exist on paper. This girl was going to be our only link to him. I've never met her and she doesn't know me, so me doing the buy was our best chance of getting any information," he said in a rush.

I raised my eyebrow skeptically. "So you expect his son's girlfriend to agree to a buy with someone she doesn't know? For someone that's been in the crew for this long, don't you find that the least bit suspicious? I mean, hell, Shane, when you were dealing would you do a buy with a stranger? Without someone introducing you?"

"No, but we're getting desperate. They've been quiet, Megs. Too quiet. With everything Henrico has told us, and going on historic trends, we should have seen a reaction from the cartel by now. But we haven't seen shit. And you wouldn't have had to worry; the taskforce was going to go in as soon as the buy was done."

"But why now? After everything we've been through, why do you have to do this now?

Shane rubbed his face in frustration. "Because, Megan, this case isn't over. Yeah, the informant we have is singing like a bird, but that doesn't mean we're free. There are factions of the cartel out there dying to get the upper hand and look good to Christian Cruz. We have no solid proof against this jackass, and he's going to stay out of jail until we do. Our family will never be safe until he's dead."

I shook my head, incredulous at the whole situation. "So it's always going to be like this? It's always going to be drug deals and sneaking behind my back and half-truths?" I gave him a sad smile. "I can't live like that."

"Dammit, Meg! You know I don't want you to live like that either, but what can I do? It's either bring the fight to them or hide at the farm, in fear, for the rest of our lives. And dammit, I protect what's mine! I almost lost you once; I'm not going to lose you again."

"It doesn't have to be you. You don't have to do this. Let the FBI do their job."

"Yes I do! I have to pay those motherfuckers back for everything they did to me. They ruined our lives. They killed Eric. They almost killed you and Katie. This is *my* retribution. This is *my* fight!"

I choked back a sob and covered my mouth with my hand. It wasn't the words or the tone that scared me the most, it was the look in his eyes. Shane's eyes burned dark with vengeance. And knowing him, he wouldn't stop until he got what he needed.

"I can't do this," I whispered as tears coursed down my cheek. "I'm done."

Shane didn't say a word. I turned and hurried down the street.

I reached an intersection and was lost in my misery when I bumped into a hard chest. "Oh, sorry," I mumbled in apology. Then I looked up. Surprise gave way to fury and I pulled back and slugged Tommy in the gut.

"Ow, Megs, what the hell?" He doubled over. My hand stung but I didn't care. It felt good to hit him.

"For having Shane do a buy and for ruining my vacation. I'm done with all this bullshit, Tommy. I'm fucking done."

I brushed past him and stalked to my SUV, digging through my purse to find my keys.

Tommy hurried after me. "Megs, wait. I'm sorry it happened while you're on vacation, but I couldn't tell him no. We needed to get it done."

"What do you mean, you couldn't tell him no? What kind of an answer is that? Are you or are you not running this case?" I whirled around and poked him in the chest. The contrite look on his face confirmed my suspicions. "Screw you, Tommy. Your work is your first priority. Who cares what happens to those involved, as long as you get credit and the bad guys get taken down."

Tommy ran his hand through his blond hair and sighed. "That's not true. Getting you was my first priority."

"Getting me? What the heck are you talking about now?" I muttered as I searched through the mess in my purse and paid him no mind. "Crap. I left my keys at the house." I didn't relish the thought of going back to Shane to get the keys, so I turned to walk down the street. *I'll just take the bus.*

"My car's right here. Do you want a ride somewhere?" Tommy leaned against the black Suburban parked next to me. I rolled my eyes and started walking. With no destination in mind, I just kept walking with the primary goal being to put more distance between Shane and me. I needed to clear my head, to think. *The asshole didn't even follow me. Some badass protector he is.*

Tommy pulled up just as I reached Coastal Highway.

"Come on, let's get a drink. I want to talk to you anyway."

A drink sounded good. In fact, copious amounts of drinks sounded even better. "I don't want to talk to you Tommy." The light turned and I took a step to cross the street when something grabbed my purse and yanked me back. Startled, I stumbled and fell into someone's arms. A sharp pinch in my neck caused me to cry out and I tried to move away, but large tanned arms gripped me tightly.

"You're not going anywhere, Megs." My body suddenly felt heavy, but I managed to turn my head toward the voice.

"Tommy?" my voice slurred and the heaviness in my legs made it impossible for me to stand. Whoever was holding me dragged me over to Tommy's SUV and tossed me in like a sack of potatoes. I struggled to keep my eyelids open and to stay coherent, but darkness took over.

CHAPTER 23

OH LORD, *I HAVE TO PUKE.*

A rocking sensation and the desperate urge to throw up woke me from the haze. I blinked slowly, and then my eyes flew open as the memories of what had happened flooded back. Tommy grabbed me. I had no idea where I was or if Shane knew what had happened. *Oh my God! Shane!* My heart jumped into my throat and I struggled to move my arms to no avail. They were tied tightly together to posts above my head. Panting, I gulped down the rising bile as the rocking motion continued.

I looked around and took in my surroundings. The plush bed on which I was tied and the shiny wood paneling on the walls screamed money. A muffled argument broke out above me and then I heard loud footsteps coming down the stairs. My pulse raced and I tried to maneuver my body off the bed, but I couldn't budge. A scream was building in my lungs but I bit my lip and squeezed my eyes shut, desperate not to announce my consciousness.

The slow creak of the door as it opened frayed each of my nerves in anticipation. Despite my best efforts not to, I trembled in fear. The mattress sank under the weight of someone sitting next to me and a rough hand brushed the hair from my face. It took everything I had not to cry out.

"Megan, it's time to wake up now. I know you can hear me," a familiar voice crooned. My gut dropped when I heard Tommy's voice. The caress of silk in his tone, often used to cajole or placate his witnesses, was like fingernails on a chalkboard.

My eyes opened slowly and I looked at my former fiancé with disgust. "Where the hell am I, Tommy? Where's Shane?"

"You wanted a vacation, right? Well, you're on vacation," he replied, helping me sit up. My hands tied awkwardly to the post left me no wiggle room, so I was forced to sit sideways, next to him. "I left Shane in Ocean City. That wasn't a real vacation anyway. Just a transit point."

I swallowed, desperate for some water, but too

frightened to ask. "What do you mean, a transit point?"

Tommy smiled and brushed another lock of my hair away. "Because, Megs, I needed to get you down here. Someone very important wants to meet you."

"Where the hell are we?"

"Miami." My fists ached to punch that smug grin off his face but, even as I struggled, the ropes around my wrists tightened. "Up you go, you have someone waiting." Keeping my hands tied together, he undid the knot on the post and brought me to my feet. Panic set in and I fought against his grip, despite my weakened state.

"No, Tommy, I don't want to meet anyone. Just let me go. Please, let me go," I pleaded, pushing back on each step.

"Oh, sweet Megan. If only your boyfriend would have listened and left well enough alone, you wouldn't be in this predicament. But noooo. He had to play the hero and not only survive that explosion, but also come back to town. Hell, even after everything that's happened since he's been back—your car accident, the fire, Rachel Morrison's death—he has still stuck around. One would think he's a glutton for punishment," Tommy sneered, the loathing clearly evident in his voice as he dragged me up the short flight of stairs.

His words shocked me to the core and turned my stomach.

"Did...were you behind all of that?" I stuttered.

Tommy smirked. "How else was I supposed to make your hero realize that he's no good for you? If he hadn't been around, none of those things would have happened. Except for Rachel. Bitch refused to keep her big fat mouth shut. Constantly moaning about seeking revenge, that her brother was set up. Her bastard brother needed to die. And she just had to follow him."

He opened the door and I was blinded by the sun's white-hot glare. Bringing my tied hands up to shield my eyes, I looked over his shoulder. The boat was moored in a marina at the last slip, from what I could tell. Tommy pulled me toward a small group of women clad in nothing but sarongs and jewels. They sat in a small cluster around a slender, older, bald man dressed in a white linen suit. Two large men in gray suits and sunglasses with heavy artillery flanked him.

The man smiled broadly at my arrival, "Megan Connors, how nice of you to join us." His smile didn't reach his cold blue eyes.

Tommy nudged me to say something, but I refused to play his game. I'd read too many suspense novels and watched too many movies to think that begging and pleading for my life would make any difference. I stood there, and stared into the eyes of the older man.

"Thomas, how rude of you. You didn't introduce us," he said with a cool glare.

Tommy coughed. "Of course. Megan, I'd like you to meet Christian Cruz, my father."

My mouth fell open and I gasped in shock. Tommy smiled in satisfaction.

"Oh, that's right. I never told you, did I? Christian Cruz is my biological father. When my parents met, my grandparents weren't fond of Dad's chosen occupation. Needless to say, they were appalled by my conception so they threatened to disown my mother if they married. It didn't help that by then he was knee-deep in dealings with the cartel and the mafias in New York. Along came Colton Thomas Greene, the rich investment broker. He was sterile and needed an heir to inherit the family fortune. Luckily for him, my mother was pregnant by a man she loved but couldn't marry. A simple business arrangement. "

"Ah yes, your grandparents. Bitter old crones," sneered Christian, leaning back in his captain's chair.

"So you're his son? The ghost no one could track?"

Tommy shrugged nonchalantly. "Only a few people know that Christian Cruz has a son. I didn't even know until my grandparents died and my mother was released from her bond of silence."

"My business dealings were becoming more prominent, shall we say, and Thomas made sure that there was never too much pressure."

"You intervened in federal cases so your father

wouldn't get caught." I didn't ask the question, just made the statement. "Why Shane?"

"Because he knew too much. He was small-time when I met him, it was pure happenstance that he caught Reggie's eye. Reggie wanted to groom him, have him became part of the family, but I couldn't have that. That blast was supposed to take care of the nuisance. But then he came back, and I thought we were toast. Thankfully, lover boy didn't know his ass from a hole in the ground. Kate and Rick had their suspicions, but no one believed them. No one knows a thing. My name is perfectly clean; there is no evidence to link me to anything." Tommy paused, then smirked.

"I tried to make you see that he was no good for you. That coming back into your life was the wrong thing for him to do. He has done nothing to make your life better. If anything, he's made it worse. I mean, hell, I made sure he missed the birth of Katie by putting something in your tea to start your labor, and yet you still take him back? What kind of masochistic bitch are you?"

My blood boiled as rage coursed through my veins. "You Goddamn son of a bitch. You put my family in danger. You put my daughter in danger. I'm going to kill you," I seethed, lunging for him. The ferocious urge to kill him was so strong. Even with my hands tied I went for his gun, but I was too addled by the drugs still flowing through my system. Tommy sidestepped me and the armed gorillas easily took me down.

"Pity. I thought you were better than that, Megs," Tommy sniffed as one of his flunkies yanked me up by my shirt collar. "And now, princess, we wait for your hero to appear. He received pictures of you in my arms shortly after we left Maryland yesterday, so we should see him in minute." Tommy gazed through Christian's binoculars, searching the horizon.

"What happens if he brings the police?" I asked. The question was ridiculous because I already knew the answer.

"Then you die." Christian responded nonchalantly. As if killing me was just that simple.

"I'm going to die regardless, right? Why don't you just do it now and get it over with?" I looked at Tommy expectantly. He kept his eyes fixed on the horizon, ignoring me and my question.

"My dear, it's not you we want. We need to teach your boyfriend a lesson. He betrayed the trust of our family. He ruined my business. The amount of money I lost because of him is quadruple what Shane is worth. But I will take his life and everything he loves as penance. He will watch you suffer, just as we have suffered for his treason to the family," Christian said softly.

I frantically moved my attention back to Tommy. "Tommy, you can't do this. I can't leave my baby without parents. Please, Tommy. Please," I begged.

Tommy finally looked at me with sadness. "You should have stayed with me, Megan. Think of the life we could have had. I tried to make you see he wasn't worth it, but you wouldn't believe me."

"A life of lies, drugs, and mayhem? Yeah, no thanks." Tears rolled down my cheeks. I desperately searched for a way off the yacht, but aside from jumping into the ocean, I had little chance of escape. *Thank God Katie is safe.* Though I was grateful that we had left her and Mom at home, the thought of her growing up without me broke my heart.

A shot rang out in the distance and Tommy shouted an order for more security. Twelve men exited from the deck below and rushed the dock. The two burly guards flanked Christian as he moved to the front of the boat. Tommy grabbed my arm and jerked me to his side. With his hand squeezing my bicep tightly, he pressed his lips against my ear and whispered, "The fireworks are about to begin."

Silent sobs racked my body as Tommy held me against him and we watched the action unfold on the shore. A Suburban squealed to a stop at the front of the dock. Amid the hail of gunfire, a lone figure emerged from the vehicle and fired back.

"Shane," I whispered.

Tommy clucked approvingly. "Bastard listened." Suddenly three more SUVs plowed their way to the dock. The exchange of gunfire kept Tommy's attention, so I surreptitiously glanced up at his face and then over his shoulder. Taking my chance, I shoved my body into him and went for the gun in his waistband. I knocked him down and almost fell with him, but somehow straightened myself out. The gun clattered to the ground and I scrambled to get it.

I pointed the gun at Tommy with my trembling tied hands. "Tommy, please! Don't make me do this."

Tommy rose from the white fiberglass floor and wiped the blood from the gash on his head. "Megan, give me the gun."

"No! I don't want to shoot you Tommy but, dammit, don't test me. I will do it."

"Give me the damn gun, Megan."

"Let me go, Tommy. Please, just let me go. I loved you once; I don't want to do this. Don't make me pull the trigger." Tears clouded my eyes as it became harder to keep the gun steady.

"Give me the fucking gun, Megan. Now!" he roared.

I disengaged the safety and fired one shot at his feet. It was supposed to be a warning, but Tommy lunged toward me at the same time I fired and landed on top of me. We fell to the ground, wrestling for the gun. A shot rang out and instantly my hip was ablaze in heat. I screamed in agony and let go of the gun.

"Megan!" Tommy cried out, rolling me on to my

side. Another shot fired, the bullet piercing my side. Shrieks of pain echoed throughout the marina. Tommy grabbed his gun and jumped up. I could barely see through my tears and the excruciating pain.

"Goddamn bastard. Why the hell did you do that?" I heard Tommy shout.

"She's trouble. Finish them both and be done with it," came a faraway voice. Christian. Tommy roared and fired four shots. The shell casings clinked when they hit the ground.

I couldn't hear anything except for the boat motor churning below. My breath slowed and came in short gasps. My body chilled in the warm sunlight and my eyes didn't want to stay open.

"Shit, Megs. I'm sorry. I'm sorry. This wasn't supposed to happen. Dammit, you screwed it up. Shane and Christian were supposed to die, not you." Tommy's warm hands slipped underneath me and lifted me up. Suspended in midair, he shouted, "Stay off the dock. You come any closer and I'll drop her in the ocean!"

Silence.

Pain overtook every nerve in my body; I couldn't move. The fog in my mind closed in and I welcomed the numbness that followed. Three more shots rang out, piercing the silence.

The last thing I heard was an agonized cry: "Megan!"

EPILOGUE

TIME FLIES.

Before I realized it, it was September. Three months have passed since our lives were turned upside down. Again. Three months since the terrifying night when my girlfriend left me in anger on the boardwalk of Ocean City and then disappeared into the night at the hands of someone we trusted. Three months since I received the text message containing a picture of the person I loved most in the world passed out with a gun to her head and the words "It's time to pay your dues."

I remember that night clearly. Her mother, holding my precious daughter, looked me dead in the eyes and said, "Bring her home, Shane." I looked at the men who I considered my brothers, helpless and shaking with rage. My first instinct was to destroy everything in sight, but Rick and Kyle managed to calm me to the point where they could talk some sense into me. Cole contacted Kate, who was already in Miami. With only a few calls, an FBI jet had arrived and was waiting for us at the Ocean City airport, ready to take us to Miami.

Thankfully, Kate's tenacity for running down the stupidest leads paid off. Unbeknownst to all of us, she had been watching Tommy since she had returned from Florida. She had finally been able to piece together the puzzle, she told us. But Tommy had taken Megan before Kate was able to bring her case to the higher-ups. With the help of her brother, Cole, we managed to track Tommy to his yacht docked in Miami.

The sound of gunfire still echoes in my head. The vivid images of that day play repeatedly in my mind: Megan struggling with Tommy, the horrific scream of agony when she was shot, the look on Tommy's face as he held her limp body in his arms. Then the terrifying moment when he dropped her body into the turquoise blue waters of the Atlantic. After that, whether Tommy was alive or dead no longer mattered. All that mattered was getting to Megan. I ran down the dock and dove into the water while Tommy's boat sped away.

We pulled her out just as the EMTs were arriving. She wasn't breathing, and she had no a pulse. The sight of her blue lips and ashen skin caused me to lose all composure. I wanted to push the EMTs out of the way, to try to save her myself, but I knew I had to let them do what they do best. I wasn't ready to give up on her, on us. Not after the hell we had gone through. After they got her heart beating again, she was airlifted to the closest trauma center, where she was stabilized. She was then flown to Johns Hopkins for further treatment.

We had survived another battle with the cartel, but we were both badly scarred. Once Megan's body began to heal, we both began the long journey to recovery. For Megan, this meant physical therapy because of the damage the bullet had done to her hip. For me, it was counseling, for which I have Kate to thank. Because of her line of work, she's familiar with the signs of PTSD, and she recommended that I see someone she trusted. At first I didn't think counseling would help; I couldn't unsee the horror I had witnessed. But as time went on, the rage and paranoia lessened. I will always protect what's mine, there's no doubt about that, but that doesn't mean that I have to constantly look over my shoulder.

Not to say that the cartel isn't a threat. They're a very real threat and I have no doubt that we'll be seeing them again. But not today. Today is a day for celebration, and I'll be damned if I'm going to let a bunch of spineless pussies ruin it.

"Dude, you ready?"

I look up at the door where my best friend, Cole, is waiting for me. I nod and stand, straightening my own slate colored tie. I take a last look in the mirror to make sure every detail is perfect. The burgundy mum and lavender sprig are firmly attached to my khaki vest. The sleeves on my shirt are rolled up so Megan's favorite tattoos are showing. Eyebrow ring and one-caret diamond earring are in place. Hair combed and facial hair groomed. Tan work boots on. Cole slaps me on my back and catches my eye in the mirror.

"She looks beautiful, man. And overjoyed to be tricked into marrying you," he says with a laugh.

I smirk. It's the joke in the family. The cartel ruined my plans to propose to Megan on the beach, but in the end it didn't matter. I didn't need to wax poetically or plan something big and elaborate. As she was coming out of anesthesia, I simply put the ring on the finger of the woman who is my world and said, "I'm never leaving your side. It's me and you, babe, until forever ends." People joke that she wasn't in her right mind, but I know, without a shadow of a doubt, that she heard and understood every single word. It was evident by her tears, her smile, and her words: "Until forever ends." Those words are etched onto my forearm and will link us for eternity.

I check the antique pocket watch Megan gave me earlier in the day. Her father gave it to her before he passed away. Inside the engraved steel box in which the watch came was a note from her father to her future husband. I shook my head, remembering the words:

> *To my future son-in-law,*
> *If you're receiving this, then you have received the honor of marrying the most precious gift I could ever give—my only daughter, Megan. She is the light of my life, my heart, my reason for breathing. She is courageous and brave, forgiving and kind. Her heart is big, so big that she sometimes doesn't see the evil that is in this world. But she chose you to love, so you already know how big and gracious her heart is. Protect her. Love her. Cherish the gift you've received.*
> *And Shane, from the first day I met you I knew you had nothing but love for Megan. You had the look—the look of absolute awe, adoration, and love. The same look I have for her mother. You're good for Megan. You'll keep her on her toes, and you'll put up with the stubbornness she gets from her mother. I put my faith in you that you will love her until the end of time. I'm proud to call you my son.*
> *William*

The man was psychic, that's for damn sure. I slip the watch back into my pocket and nod to Cole. "It's time for her to make an honest man out of me."

The warm late-September weather, with the changing leaves and a hint of fall in the air, is the perfect backdrop for today's event. With the rolling acres and an expansive creek that leads to the West River, Hollow Creek Meadows is the ideal place for a wedding. I glance around the property and smile. The faded red barn glows brightly with white lights. Long wooden tables beautifully decorated with pumpkins, mums, and sunflowers sit ready for the guests who are mingling about, holding mason jars full of freshly made apple cider and homebrewed beer from Kyle's own supply. The caterers—and by caterers I mean Megan's aunt, Karen, and her small crew of chefs—busily set up a buffet with appetizers and dishes.

The sounds of the acoustic guitar fill the air as the guests file into the rows of white chairs. Megan's Uncle Bob, the man who got me out of so many jams with the law, is officiating and stands proudly at the head of the aisle under the massive weeping willow tree. Cole, Adrian, and Rick stand beside me. As the tones of Pachelbel's Canon fly from the guitarist's fingertips, the bridesmaids slowly make their way down the aisle: Kate, Jen, Lauren, and a newly pregnant Sarah, who is also carrying my beautiful daughter down the aisle.

The music heightens and everyone stands. At the top of the aisle is my reason for breathing. Megan is beautiful, the epitome of everything that's right in the world. Her grace, her kindness, her smart-ass sense of humor—I'm the luckiest bastard in the world to be able to marry her. And I intend to show her every day how much I cherish her.

Norah and Kyle each take one of her arms to support her as she makes her way down to me. With each step she takes, my heart races. Her chocolate-brown eyes glisten with tears and her steps are shaky, but her strength still shines through. Once they get close, I can't stand it any longer and I walk up to meet them. Norah kisses my cheek with a laugh, and Kyle claps me on the back, then he joins the other men who are my brothers in everything but name.

"You look absolutely breath-taking," I whisper, cupping her delicate face in my hands.

"You're looking pretty hot yourself," she says softly and smiles.

"I love you, so much." I gently brush away the tears from her cheeks and press my lips against hers, then sweep her into my arms and walk the final steps to where we will say our vows.

After repeating our vows, the vows that have been said for generations, I wrap my arms around Megan and crush my lips to hers, dipping her in an embrace. The guests roar with cheers, and I carry my beloved bride back down the aisle through a shower of rose petals and bubbles.

The reception flies by and the air is thick with love and happiness. Gone is the tension, the stress, the fear. We are alive. And we're together. Our love has been through hell and back—and has survived. Not many people can say that. As the night comes to an end, I pull Megan into one last final dance. The song "God Bless the Broken Road" by Rascal Flatts is fitting and describes our love as well as the journey we had to take to find our love.

Megan and I are soul mates. Everyone knows it. It just took us longer to realize it for ourselves. We had to travel the broken road until we found each other.

The End

ACKNOWLEDGMENTS

Oh, holy cow. What a year this has been. The support I've received from people has been astronomical. I don't think I would have continued chasing my dream if it had not been for the help and love of some very awesome people.

Brian—*Thank you. You are the best husband ever. You pushed me and encouraged me to finish this. Thank you for your love, support, and the occasional chocolate turnover. You mean everything to me, and I love you so much.*

My Team: Carla, Robin, Emma and Cassy - —*Thank you so much for your patience, guidance, and pure awesomeness. We're a great team and I'm so glad you all took a chance on me!*

William, James and Sara – *Thank you for making both the front and back covers amazing!*

Fallon, Jason, April, Eryn, and Heather—*Again, you guys were my sounding boards. Thanks for bringing me back to earth when I had the world's worst ideas and for giving me the reality checks I always needed.*

Steve — *Thanks for putting up with my incessant police questions. I hope I did you proud.*

My family, friends, and coworkers — *I couldn't have done this without your love and support. Thank you for listening and helping me when I was stuck on the details. Xoxo.*

To my M&M chicks — *The best group of mamas I've ever been with. Thanks for listening, caring, and being there for me at all hours of the night.*

My crew – *Kathryn, Emma, Cassy, Tyf, Natacha, Judi, Paulette and Jen S – Your continued awesomeness and support is amazing. I truly love you all.*

My Street Team – Traci, Lizette, and Jenny – thank you for everything you do. You're truly the master pimpers! I love you hookas!

Last but not least — OMG! my readers! HOLY COW! I have the best readers in the world. You guys kept me on task, kept me honest, and pushed me to finish the book. Without your encouragement and support, I wouldn't have gotten this far. Thank you for your patience. This book is for you. Xoxoxoxo.

ABOUT THE AUTHOR

Melissa grew up in Maryland by the Chesapeake Bay, where her favorite memories took place near the water. Now she lives near Washington, D.C. with her family, dog, and a lot of fish. In between the chaos of laundry, chasing after her three children and trying not to burn dinner, Melissa continues to find her escape by feeding her addiction of reading and writing about love, suspense, and humor.

Melissa loves to hear from readers! She can be contacted at:

Email — melissa@melissahuie.com
Website — www.melissahuie.com
Twitter — www.twitter.com/melissahuie
Facebook — www.facebook.com/melissadhuie
Goodreads — www.goodreads.com/melissa_huie